Praise for *T*

"I loved it! I've known a surprising number of kids like Alexa, but—like so many great stories—this story made me think of myself. It felt so _real_. Funny, touching, full of ideas and information that were at once new and yet familiar, this is a book that children and their parents can all enjoy—and _relate_ to. Anyone who knows me knows I love "geeky" people. Schultz takes a year from the life of Alexa, written in Alexa's ten-year-old voice, and spins a tale so lively, real and poignant that it will linger with me for a very long time. I can't wait to recommend it to my clients, my relatives, and my friends. Will this be a series?"

— Deborah L. Ruf, Ph.D., Author of *Five Levels of Gifted*
Founder: EducationalOptions.com, TalentIgniter.com

"A poignant story of a gifted ten-year-old girl and her friends and family, The Howling Vowels *begs for its pages to be turned as Alexa experiences life with unbridled enthusiasm. With the special relationship between Alexa and her parents firmly planted at the heart of the story, Schultz tells of escapades with friends that will appeal to young readers and very likely inspire them to embark on their own amazing learning adventures. The voices of the children ring true within the book's authentic dialogue. Young people will enjoy this book—and their parents will, too—as it entertains, inspires, and informs!*"

— Bonnie Jean Flom, Public School Teacher,
Principal, and Educational Consultant

"The Howling Vowels *contains four vividly drawn seasons, a year of transforming adventures with Alexa and her friends, and a generous dollop of humor. Leslie Schultz is a poet with a full and burning heart for the beauty of the world. Alexa's adventures in Sun Dog bring the people lucky enough to live in Leslie's world to life. Honestly, I wish I lived there myself.*"

— Caroline Stevermer, Author of *Magic Below Stairs*
members.authorsguild.net/carolinestev/

The Howling Vowels

Written by Leslie Schultz

Illustrated by Heather Newman

Printed in the United States of America

First Printing, 2011

ISBN: 0-9824829-7-3
ISBN-13: 978-0-9824829-7-1
Library of Congress Control Number: 2011940591

Published by Do Life Right, Inc.
P.O. Box 61
Sahuarita, AZ 85629

www.DoLifeRightInc.com

Visit **www.DoLifeRightInc.com** to order additional copies or
e-mail sales@doliferightinc.com to inquire about bulk and
wholesale discounts.

Visit **www.winonamedia.net** to find out
more about Leslie Schultz.

Dedicated to all the kids
who feel different, special, weird,
amazing, and cool.

You are—in or out of school.

Leslie Schultz
Author

The Howling Vowels

ISBN 9780982482971
authors@winonamedia.net
www.winonamedia.net

*For **Tim** and **Julia**,*
the alpha and omega of my domestic heart;
you always believe in me,
make me laugh,
and cheer me on,
so this story is for you.
- Leslie

ABUNDANT THANKS TO:

I've found that it takes a village to homeschool a child, launch a business, write a book, or do just about anything worthwhile. I am so incredibly fortunate in being part of a web of wonderful, supportive people strung across time and space—some near, some far, some never met. Long as it is, this list is far too short! May we all have grateful hearts. Be certain that many people appreciate you for kind words or deeds you don't remember.

     - Leslie Schultz

Karla Schultz, my beautiful, generous sister, always an inspiration to me;
Jane Schultz, my mother, a creative lady, and my first teacher;
Richard Schultz, my father, who enjoyed silliness and making things;
The Wardens, Aunt Shirley, Uncle Bill, Carolyn, Bill, great cheerleaders;
Ann Lacy, whose keen eye and kindness have helped me for 30 years;
Pat Kaluza, astrologer *par excellence* and dear friend;
Caroline Stevermer, a writer of wit, elegance, and force, and a role model;
E. Ryan "The Lion" Edmonds, a great-hearted friend alive to every nuance;
Laura, **Atia**, **Liana**, **Julia**, and **Eugenia**, the girls of the Literature Enhancement Society, for sharing your joy of writing;
Kate Stuart & **Lisa Olson**, friends and homeschooling moms who teach me;
Julia & **Nina Denne**, who understand the powers of myth and literature;
Sally Nacker, an irreplaceable friend of the work and also of the heart;
Julia Uleberg Swanson, who is always there when she is needed;
Corinne & **Elvin**; **Rich** & **Raymonde**; **Catherine**, **Atango**, & **Kelsi**; **Janet**, **Joel**, & **Ben**; **Josie**, **Stephen**, **Cricket**, & **Piper**; **Lin** & **Bob**; **Barbara**, **Bob**, **Tim**, & **Jennifer**; **David**, **Jennifer**, **Sylvia**, & **Anders**; **Tony** & **Loretta**; **Marty**, **Matt**, & **Martha**; **Deane** & **Ian**; the **Weber-Young** and **Artley families**—strong threads in the fabric of our town;
Susan Hvistendahl, who first introduced me to *El Día de los Muertos*;
DeWayne and **Theo Wee**, exemplars not only of piano but of joy in life;
Sarah Stensrud, better known to thousands of kindergarteners as Ms. Sarah, for providing a wonderful year of public school for Julia;
Ellen Keller, who teaches me to keep the edge of childhood sharply honed;
Sandra Petrek, whose wisdom and grace are a daily example;

LaNelle Olson, who took a chance on me and changed my life;

Bonnie Jean Flom, thank you for walks, talks, laughs, hugs, and shared adventures (and the original of *Bonnie and the Clydes*);

Jan Newman, Beth Clary, Myrna Mibus & Azna Amira, talented writers all;

Jan & Bob Davidson and their amazing staff at the **Davidson Institute for Talent Development**—thank you for your vision, commitment, practical help & moral support;

Deborah Ruf—thank you for your expertise & inspiration;

Lynne Young and the staff of the Northfield Public Library—you are the high priestesses of literature and exemplars of public service;

Northfield's Arts & Culture Commission for their unique blend of idealism and practicality which makes our city an even better place for artists to live and work;

Roxanne Heaton, Marie Marvin, Bunny Lance, Jill Ewald, & Bob Bowman, thanks for your faith in my visual arts side;

Marilyn Larson, Lynda Grady, & Patsy Dew, thanks for shared creativity;

Susan Showalter, thank you for your smile;

Carol Harris, whose friendship and good cheer mean so much to me;

Gretchen Falck for *Forza! Fit*, which makes me stronger and braver;

Marla Cilley, a.k.a. Flylady, whose online encouragement has greatly improved my home life and given me more time to write. Your courage gives me wings;

Ellen Whitehurst and **Nancy SantoPietro**—feng shui gurus who have mightily assisted my work, life, health, & happiness;

Paramahansa Yogananda, whose life is an example of prolific creativity and peace;

Michael Clay Thompson, for your wonderful writing curricula;

Garrison Keillor, true champion of poetry and storytelling;

and for

Maud Hart Lovelace, L. M. Montgomery, and **Laura Ingalls Wilder** for enriching my life beyond measure. Your examples showed me where to begin.

Table of Contents

1. Bridge Square
2. Sunday Public Library
3. Alexa's house
4. Otto's house
5. Central Park
6 Eduardo's house
7 Isabelle's house
8 Birchwood College
9 Ursula's house
10 Islands in the Stream
11 Hospital
12 Miss Arnold's house
13 Professors Davenport's house
14 St Angelina's church
15 Miss Ann's house
16 Arts Guild

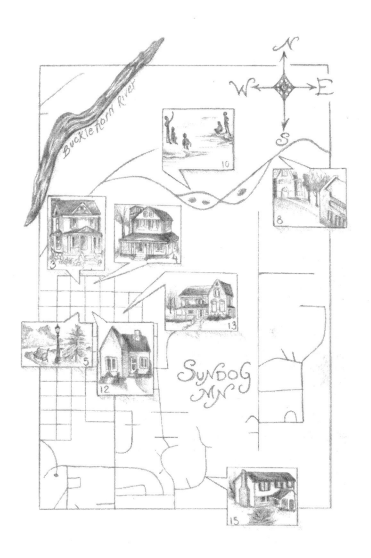

Chapter One
"Alexa Alone"

A lexa Stevens here with a special late-breaking news bulletin from Sundog, Minnesota. Sundog, a small college town about an hour south of the Twin Cities, has been overrun—repeat!—overrun by a roving band of imaginative children. Calling themselves The Howling Vowels, this gangly gang is so bent on finding fun and discovering new words that they will even synthesize both.

Like lone atoms joined by shifting covalent bonds into a hitherto unknown morphing molecule this cluster of children has been partially identified by the letters "A," "E," "I," "O," and "U." Only one thing has been observed to stop their free-wheeling verbal antics: tasty snacks. All households are being advised to stock up now—I repeat! Now!—on primary food groups to deploy at a moment's notice.

Oh, wait.

You are probably wondering where this is going. To explain, I really better start at the beginning...

My name is Alexa Stevens. Now I am ten years old and live in the Midwest, but until last year I used to live in a big co-op building on the upper west side of

Manhattan in New York City. A co-op is like an apartment building except that everyone owns their living space, instead of renting it, so it is sort of like having lots of houses stacked on top of each other.

There are so many people in New York City, and they all live so close together that you wouldn't think it would be possible to be lonesome. But think again. Now everything is different. I might be weird in some ways but I have found some good friends who like me anyway. And guess what? I like myself, too, now. It wasn't always easy, though.

My troubles started when I was five years old.

Okay, like a lot of kids, I was nervous about starting kindergarten because I had just turned five when school began. Still, I liked meeting the other kids. I loved my teacher, Ms. Suzie. For six months, I even stopped reading and just played all day. But in first grade I started having problems in school. Probably not like you think. People think all kinds of things about NYC, I've learned. But school was *way* too easy. Too safe. I mean, they wanted me to spell "cat, mat, rat." Over and over. Even "latitude" and "atmosphere" weren't challenging "at" words for me. In first grade, I had three teachers instead of one. Math was $1 + 1 = 2$. And science was pretty lame, too, just "head, body, fin" instead of "cephalothorax" or "contour feather." After a few weeks, I was desperate for some new information. My brain felt starved.

Mom tried to talk to the teachers. At first, they said, "Challenges will come," and "Her handwriting is very shaky," and "Socialization is exceedingly important, as are our routines." At Miss Prescott's Day School they are *quite firm* about many things, including hand hygiene. (Now this is something I agree with, though I do forget sometimes.) My stomach hurt a lot. I only looked forward to music, recess, lunch, and gym, when I could play with my friends. But then that changed, too.

In kindergarten, I got to sit next to twins, Maddie and Sage. So what if they were a little slow with the alphabet? It didn't bother me. But after kindergarten, Sage started hating me. The more trouble she had with reading, the more mean things she said to me.

I said, "Hey, I can help you learn new words. It's fun!"

She said, "You're weird."

Then, one day, Janie Murphy warned me that Sage was waiting for me on the playground with a big ice ball hidden in her pocket. She said Sage wanted to brain me with it. So I knew that our friendship was now out of the question, but I didn't know why. Mom and Dad couldn't tell me either. I think they were puzzled, too.

Maybe I should tell you a little bit about my parents and me.

I am tall for my age and have green-grey eyes and reddish-gold hair. Sometimes I am really intense and sometimes I am really silly. I don't like to sit still for too long.

Mom is curvy and comfortable and likes fashion. She is an artist and a word person. She has green eyes and a great laugh.

Dad grew up on a farm. He is big and shaggy and tells long, hilarious stories, but he doesn't laugh very often. His hair and eyes and moustache are all brown, like a buffalo, and he has the biggest, strongest arms you ever saw. He is mostly a math person, but he knows the lyrics to every rock and roll song written before 1983.

They both tried to help me with the weirdness and uncomfortableness at school. Dad let me read to him from encyclopedia volumes and anatomy books. He took me to the soccer park, and one clear day we walked all the way across the Brooklyn Bridge to a concert at BAM, the Brooklyn Academy of Music. On the cab ride back we imitated all the odd, squeaky, clunky sounds that made up the music.

Mom was already walking with me to school every day, and she started to stick around, volunteering in my class. I guess she saw what I was up against firsthand, because one Saturday (when they thought I was drawing in my room) I heard Mom and Dad talking in the living room. I knew it was about me, so I crept into the hall and held my breath quiet.

"She is so unhappy," Mom said.

"She used to sing and dance all the time," said Dad.

A few weeks later, Mom took me to the office of a really nice lady, Dr. Nadine Rudolph. She had golden hair and very alert eyes. She gave me all kinds of tests that were totally fun. Afterwards, I felt very energized and zingy. I got to do one test at home. It was all about the things I prefer. For example, did I like being in a big noisy birthday party (*not!*), or sitting in a boat on a quiet lake? Well, I don't know anything about boats, but there were no right answers, just my answers. To tell you the truth, lots of questions didn't have anything close to "my" answer at all, so I just tried to select the one closest. Like if I had a choice between two activities: I would choose the quiet one every time, so I picked the lake.

These tests helped me learn some amazing things about myself. I learned that I am an introvert. That means that I feel overwhelmed if I am with too many noisy people all day. I like to make noise and talk a lot, but I don't feel energized by blaring music or crowds. That's what extroverts like. Introverts like me need to "turn in" to ourselves pretty often or we feel overwhelmed.

I also learned that I am something called "profoundly gifted," which means I am waaaay over at the end of the bell curve, in the last 99.9th percentile. So my brain needs lots of new information every day. I learned that I am verbal and "gifted in fluid reasoning." That means I think on my feet. Mom and Dad say it means I would be a good lawyer, because I like to quibble and find loopholes and exceptions for everything they say. I learned that I am pretty good in math, but not fabulous-fantastic in it. And I learn really well if I can move around and ask questions right away. Basically, I realized that I am just myself. There is nothing wrong with me. But that there aren't so very many people like me, and so the world isn't set up for my kind.

Here is another interesting fact I learned: there are three extroverts for every introvert. And here's something else: people who think fast like me are about one in 10,000. Most of these one-in-10,000 are boys who are really into math and computers. I want to do so many different things it makes my head spin, but I hardly ever want to do math. Talking is what I like.

At first, it made me feel lonely to think that there aren't many kids like me, especially not many girls like me. I felt like Sage was right. I *was* weird. Then I realized that *no one* is just like me, and I keep changing, too. And, hey, that is true for everyone!

Right then, I knew that someday I would find a special friend, and chances are she'd be very different from me. I was right. And wrong. I found four great friends: two boys and two girls, and no two alike.

When Mom and Dad went to get the test results in a conference with Dr. Rudolph, I got to hang out with Señor Raoul for an hour. He is the doorman in our old building and my special friend. He and his wife live in the apartment closest to the front door, just to the right as you come in the lobby.

Señor Raoul and I like to talk about Mexico, a place he knows well, and about Central and South America. I want to visit all these places some day. He tells me about the *cadejos*, the magic dogs who live on the slopes of the volcanoes and eat morning glory seeds, and about the ancient Mayans and Aztecs and Incas, and about the people who even today live on reed islands and float their whole lives in the middle of Lake Titicaca.

Señora Raoul brought us a plate of crispy cookies dusted with cinnamon sugar. She arranged them with slices of fruit. She always wears the most elegant high heels. That day her green shoes were made of tooled leather.

When Mom and Dad returned, they looked unhappy and happy at the same time.

"Hi, Kitten," said Dad. He opened up his arms to scoop me up.

"Thank you, so much, Señor Raoul," said Mom.

"*De nada*. It's okay. We pass the time berry well." Señor Raoul speaks excellent English, but I can still hear the echo of Mexico in his Vs.

"*Hasta luego*, Señor Raoul," I said, wiping the sugar from my lips with the back of my hand. I pushed the elevator button with my elbow. I like to do that. I closed my eyes and concentrated. Soon I could hear the grinding of the elevator cables high up in the shaft. Pretty soon the doors opened and we all stepped in.

Once the door closed, I began to tap dance. I love the feeling of tap dancing while the elevator is rising up, just like a stage in an old MGM movie. Also, moving around helps me when I feel nervous. There wasn't a lot of room, but I can do a lot in a small space. Once I even tapped my whole routine in the broom closet, just to see if I could do it. When I saw that the elevator was almost at our floor, I did the splits just as the door opened. Then I leapt up.

Naturally, I was the first one to reach number 1219, our door. Sometimes I like to think I am going so fast that sparks are spinning around my heels. Lately, though, I am a lot better about looking at where I am going, ever since that unfortunate incident when I slammed into Mrs. Harrison and she dropped all her groceries. I felt bad about it, but it was interesting to see how the oranges all rolled to the right side of the hall. There must be a very slight slant in the floor. Maybe back when they built the subway line, the front half of the building began to sink a little. I know that Manhattan rests on granite, but what if slow-acting, granite-eating bacteria were recently released from the earth's core through the hot water vents on the floor of the sea, and because of global warming, these bacteria have migrated to the Hudson River and are even now nibbling away at the bedrock? Then, by 10,000 C.E. or so, our building might look like the Leaning Tower of Pisa.

Anyway, I did feel upset about knocking into Mrs. Harrison, even though she was pretty nice about it.

Now, if I see anyone in the hall, I just "hasten my stride." That is not quite running. Mom made a ruling on it. She said it squeaked in under the wire on a technicality.

Once we were all inside, I bombarded Mom and Dad with questions. "So, what did Dr. Rudolph say? Can I see her again? I like her; did she like me? Did you know that Señor Raoul taught me some more words in Spanish?"

"Hold your horses, A," said Dad. "Why don't you go wash your hands and let us get dinner started?"

"*Magnifico!*" I answered. I was suddenly starving. But as I turned on the water, I got a little nervous. What if there was something they didn't want to tell me? So I turned the water down to a tiny trickle, and I opened the bathroom door, and I stuck one ear out into the hall.

Mom and Dad were rinsing and chopping. The refrigerator door opened and closed. The hot oil hissed as Mom threw something fresh into it. Good smells began to drift down the hall. I could hear just a little.

"Mumble, mumble, school, mumble," said Mom.

"New York regulations, mumble, sigh," said Dad.

"Alexa is flexible, and mumble. Work from home if mumble," said Mom.

"Mumble saw this coming. Mumble, mumble, curve ball, mumble, take it in stride," said Dad.

My hands were getting all pink and wrinkly. I turned off the water and dried them on the towel, then opened the door all the way and marched into the kitchen.

"Hey," I said. "You're talking about me, and I can't understand what you are saying. I should get to hear this stuff."

Mom and Dad looked at each other. Mom nodded a little. She put a lid on the skillet, pulled out a kitchen chair and sat down. Then she pulled me onto her lap.

Dad said, "Well, A, we all know that your school is a good one. But we also know that it hasn't been a good fit."

I nodded.

"And we arranged these tests with Dr. Rudolph to help us think about what kind of education would be best for you."

"Dad," I interrupted, climbing off Mom's lap. "This isn't exactly a news flash here."

"Right. Well, Dr. Rudolph recommends a tailored curriculum, a program of studies designed just for you."

"Wow!" I did a little dance. "Just for me? Like, I could study what is interesting and skip the rest?"

"Not exactly," said Mom with a little smile. "More like your school work would be designed to challenge you without giving you too much busy work. So you'd still have to work on penmanship and mathematics..."

I sighed really big, sat down, and let my head clunk onto the table.

Mom just continued on, "...but you would be able to ask questions and go deeper into the subjects that captured your interest. You would have more options for structuring your time. You wouldn't have to stop just when you were getting started simply because the bell rang."

"This sounds like a *great* school!" I shouted. "Where is it? What is it called?"

"Well, Lexi, this would be a different experience. Tailor made. We would homeschool, so Daddy and I would be your teachers."

I know I did a double take, because Mom and Dad both laughed at me. Then I laughed, too. "Woo-hoo!" I shouted and zoomed around the kitchen. Then I stopped and did a little jig. Well, maybe a sailor's hornpipe. I was so happy.

And I mostly stayed happy. Mom and I tried to spend most mornings on schoolwork, and then we went out in the afternoons. We got to see a lot of museums, which I love. If you visit when it isn't so busy, you get to ask lots more questions. I *love* to ask questions. We also got to walk through Central Park for gym class some days. I kept going to my tap dance class, and Mom signed me up for tai kwon do and ballet. Actually, she went a little overboard with outside activities, if you ask me. I think she was afraid that I would be bored all alone with just her, which would *not* be the case, but anyway, I got to go to chess club, and a mother-daughter book club at the New York Library, and to a meeting of the

Latin Classics League. We got to tour the historical site of Ellis Island and visit the United Nations. One week, Dad took some vacation time and we went south to Virginia. At Colonial Williamsburg, a living history museum, I got to imagine that I was walking the streets of Virginia's capital during the Revolutionary War, and I got to stir a big black kettle of soap while wearing a pinner, a cap that women wore hundreds of years ago.

For two years, this is how I went to school. I had a lot of fun, and I learned a lot, too. I didn't get to play very much with other kids, though, and sometimes I really missed that. Truthfully, I was kind of lonely.

Then before Christmas the year I was nine years old, Mom and I did a big unit on Yuletide customs around the world. We spent a few afternoons making paper chains and other decorations, and then spent the morning of the winter solstice skating at Rockefeller Plaza before coming home to sip hot cocoa. Just when we were settled in, talking about Robert Frost's poem, *Stopping by Woods on a Snowy Evening*, we heard Dad's key in the lock.

"Daddy!" I cried before launching myself into a big hug around his knees. "You're home early!"

"Yep. Hi, Lexi, darling." He gave me a kiss on the top of my head, just like he always does, put down his briefcase and laptop, then took off his coat. I always felt happy to see his coat hanging on his hook, the one closest to the front door.

"Hello, Paul," said Mom. She gave him a long hug, then looked at him with that let's-not-say-too-much-now look that parents sometimes give each other when kids are around. "How did it go?"

"It was interesting. Kitten, I got you a new book on Norse myths." He handed me a paper bag from the bookstore I love: McGonigle's.

"Wow! Thanks, Dad." I could tell something was up, but his strategy was sound. Norse myths were just right for snow and ice. I pulled *Tales of the Nine Worlds* by Barbara Valour out of the pale blue bag and started reading. Mom steered me by the shoulders down the hallway, and I was turning the pages before I turned into my bedroom. Mom closed the door, and I flopped on top of the bed. When I finished the introduction, I sighed with satisfaction. This was going to be a good read.

I jumped off the bed to give Dad an extra thank-you hug, but when I opened the door something made me slide down the hall in my quiet-sock way. I didn't exactly mean to be sneaky, but I remembered that something was up and I really wanted to know what it was. But it was no good; they were just sitting quietly.

"Hi," I said, as I nestled under Mom's arm.

"Hi, there," said Dad. "Alexa, your mom and I were just talking about an opportunity for our family."

"Is it a big change? Like homeschooling was?"

"Yes, it is." Dad rubbed his forehead and removed his glasses for a moment, then settled them back on his nose. "You know that I was born in Minnesota, and I grew up on a farm."

"Sure."

"Well, it was a big shock to me when I got off the Greyhound bus here in New York City. I wasn't sure if I would even make it through my first year at Columbia. Then Grandma and Grandpa moved to Florida, and I met your mom. I have learned to love this crowded, noisy, amazing place. Meeting your mother had a lot to do with that. But now I have been here twenty years. I need the fresh air, some open fields nearby. Your mother is willing to give it a try, and we think it would be good for you, too."

"So, are we going to be pioneers or something? Will we have horses?"

Mom laughed. "Well, no. Daddy has a chance to start a new software company with Vance Weber."

"His high school friend?" I looked at Dad, who nodded.

Mom continued, "We've decided to move to a small town called Sundog. It is about forty miles from the biggest cities in Minnesota: Minneapolis and Saint Paul. They are known as the Twin Cities because they are just across the Mississippi River from each other."

"Will your work be in Sundog, Dad?"

"A lot of it," Dad confirmed, then added, "I will drive into the Twin Cities about once a week. Sometimes I will have to travel to the west coast or the east coast, but most of the time I can work from an office at home."

"What about Mom? What about her studio?"

"Depending on the house we choose, Mom might be able to have a studio at home. Otherwise, she'll be able to rent a studio downtown. Sundog is developing a reputation as an arts town. That's one reason we've decided to move there."

"What about all the great things in New York?"

Mom smiled at me. She looked a bit sad, I thought. "I know how you feel," she said.

Then Dad said, "I think we'll all miss the city. But there's phone and e-mail. I've told Mom that we will definitely return for visits, at least once a year. And we will continue to subscribe to the *New York Times* and *The Wall Street Journal*."

"Don't forget *The New Yorker*, Paul."

I put my head on Mom's shoulder. She kissed me right on the top of my head.

"This must be a bit of a shock, honey," Mom said.

"That about covers it, Mom."

I really didn't know what to think. But the more I thought about it, the less sure I was. Have you seen those cartoon maps? The ones that show the east coast full of detail and the same with the west coast, while the center of the country is just a blank blur, like *terra incognita* to the Age of Discovery explorers like Vasco de Gama? That's what I thought. Except I was just ignorant then.

The next few weeks passed quickly. I got to visit Aunt Lucy in Atlanta for five days while Mom and Dad made an advance visit to Sundog to set up bank accounts and look for a house. They came back even more excited about Sundog. All they could talk about was what an adventure we were going to have in Minnesota. I still wasn't sold, but I tried not to mope and sigh. Hey, it wouldn't do any good—I could see that. And basically I am a cheerful person.

I helped to pack all our things, and I took pictures of all the places in New York I love. All the people, too, even the ones to whom I hadn't been formally introduced, like the old guy at the newsstand, and the lady who helped us at the Central Park stables.

All too soon, Dad had purchased a used minivan and loaded it full of our essential things. I mean, to the gills. He could hardly see out the back window. A moving van double-parked in front of our building for three hours, and then it drove off again. It seemed so sad to be in our apartment with only the smell of cleaning fluid and a roll of toilet paper in the bathroom that I didn't really mind going. It wasn't our home anymore, just a shell, like the casings of those insects I read about that come every seventeen years in Minnesota, the ones that make lots of loud noise and then literally climb out of their skins and go off somewhere. Our apartment was a lifeless husk, and so I was glad to strap myself into that rusty, dusty van with a bag of Señora Raoul's cinnamon cookies and start looking at the road maps.

Four days later, on a chilly February Thursday, after stops at the Liberty Bell in Philadelphia and the Chicago Museum of Science and Industry, our new-to-us minivan stopped in front of a house on Cherryvale Street. I just sat, for a moment, and looked at it, because I knew I would never again see it through stranger's eyes. It was three stories tall and had a big front porch with lots of windows. The paint was greyish blue with different colors on the trim: dark blue, dark purple, and white. The sky was bright blue and the ground was covered with fresh snow. On both sides of the front steps there were matching shrubs, each bent under the weight of the heavy, white snow. A red brick path linked the city sidewalk to the front steps. There were three shiny brass numbers to the left of the front door: 1-1-4. A big mailbox, the kind you see along country roads, was attached to the right. I wondered which windows belonged to my room.

Just then I heard the groaning of truck gears, and the big orange moving van drew up behind us. It parked with a squeak and a loud hiss, like a dragon, before it shuddered into silence. We were here, and so was all our stuff.

I got out of the van. As I closed the door, I saw a curtain twitch behind a window on the first floor of the house across the street. Then I saw a head topped with dark curls peek out under the white lace. The child smiled and then popped back under the curtain, just like a prairie dog disappearing down its hole. It all happened so quickly that I wasn't sure if I had seen a girl or a boy, or even if it had been a child my own age. But it gave me a hopeful feeling. Maybe life in Minnesota wouldn't be so dull after all.

And it wasn't. The Midwest wasn't a blank desert of snow after all. It was more like that cartoon of a scientist who writes a complicated equation on the board and right in the middle chalks "And then a miracle happens!" And the miracle was…you guessed it: friends!

Chapter Two
"Reels and Jigs"

Have you ever seen a sundog? You can only see them on extremely cold days. It's easier if you squint. They look like little rainbow-colored parentheses framing the sun. I saw my first pair on March 1st, and I remember it because that was the day I first met Otto, even though, as it turned out, he lives right across the street. I guess they named our town Sundog because it is cold here a lot but it is pretty, too.

We had been in Sundog for one week exactly, and boy, did Mom have things figured out. We were completely unpacked by day two, and Mom had decided to locate her studio in our house, at least until spring, so that was unpacked on day three. We had also gotten acquainted with the Sundog topography by making trips to all three grocery stores, the hardware store, and the public library. We had the best pizza place in town on speed dial, and we knew that Mom's special restaurant-style gas cook stove would be connected later in the week. We'd even visited the art museum on the

Birchwood College campus and looked in at the local arts guild.

The Sundog City Arts Guild was housed mainly in a narrow storefront on Sundog's Main Street. Once, long ago, it had held the public library, which had moved to a new Carnegie building across the street in 1909. On our first visit, Mom had snagged a list of classes. Now, we were heading down the stairs to the dance studio. I was signed up to take a class in Irish step dance. To be completely honest, I was pretty nervous.

The dance studio was long and skinny. Tucked under the Main Street sidewalk, to the left of the stairs, was a kitchen. In the studio, the wall to the right held a tired old piano and a row of windows. Across the room was a wall of mirrors—punctuated by a ballet *barre*. At the far end stood a big sound system, a supply closet, and a hallway that led to the elevator, the bathroom, and the door to the riverfront. The floor was a slippery blond wood that looked just perfect for sock skating. And in the middle of the floor, bowing to his reflection in the long mirrors, was a petite boy with snapping black eyes, black shiny curls, and smooth black jazz shoes on his feet. He was dressed in blue, and he could tell we were there. I know because he rose from his low bow and made a few amazing leaps and twirls, then landed, laughing, right in front of us.

We laughed back. Mom clapped. "You're great," I said.

"Thanks," he replied.

At that moment, the teacher came down the stairs, followed by three other people, students, it looked like: one tall blonde girl, one short blonde girl, and a very tall girl with black curls. Later I learned their names were Pam, Patsy, and Zinny. The boy was Otto, Zinny's younger brother.

The teacher was named Laura Hogan. She dressed like she knew the street fashion of New York firsthand and had combined it with a splash of Hello Kitty. Laura was very friendly and loved to laugh. She welcomed me and told me that she had started studying Irish step when she was six years old. Now she did all kinds of dance—jazz, tap, and modern—in between waiting on tables, but Irish was still her favorite. Laura told me not to be nervous. She said that the steps were complicated at first, but that I would soon get the hang of it. She promised to make me a CD of the music so I could practice at home. I liked her right away.

Mom was still waiting, just to see if I was going to be okay, I guess. I gave her a wave that meant, "See you at the library after class." Sometimes it is hard to know which is better—to have Mom on hand or to have privacy.

After she left, Laura called the class to order. We began warming up our muscles, the way dancers always do: rolling our necks and shoulders, stretching the hamstrings. Then Laura pushed some buttons on her iPod, which was connected by a cord to the big sound system in the corner. Something lively, with penny whistles and drums streamed out. Laura put her hands on her hips, cocked her head one way, pointed her right foot the other way, and we were off.

In a few minutes, I was hot, laughing, discouraged, and determined. I was very glad that Mom had left. These other kids had it down cold. I felt like I was jumping over puddles, and it was fun, but my feet couldn't duplicate what I was seeing others do. Fortunately, I knew from the other forms of dance I've studied that at first it is always like this, like trying to shuffle playing cards while wearing oven mitts. And I remembered what my first tap teacher, Miss Penny, always told us: we were like ducks, we should keep our faces relaxed, smile, look straight ahead, and just keep moving our feet furiously, and the dance would go forward.

I did keep making mistakes, but the other kids were nice about it. We took lots of water breaks at the drinking fountain near the kitchen. Zinny was the oldest, an eighth grader, and she gave me a thumbs up on my last skip-two-three.

When we were cooling down, kind of stretching in reverse, Laura told us that she had some news.

"Sundog is putting on a St. Patrick's Day parade this year, the first ever," she said. "The Sundog City Arts Guild has been asked to take part. The theater group and the children's arts classes are teaming up to build a float. And they have asked us to dance in front of them. It is really short notice, but I told them I would ask you. I think we can do it. What do you think?"

Everyone else gave a big cheer. I felt a bit green around the gills. "Um, Laura," I said.

"Yes, Alexa?" she asked.

"I don't think I can learn anything well enough in the next two weeks to be performing in public. Maybe you should count me out."

"Don't worry, I have an idea," she said, with a smile. Laura walked in her springy dancer's way over to the cupboard and pulled out a long wooden flag pole. As she unrolled it, I could see a bright green shamrock on a white background.

"I made this last year for the big celebration in St. Paul," she announced. "You have that traveling step down already. You can walk in front, holding this."

I smiled a lot. Now that was something I could manage. Imagine being in a parade in my new town the first month I lived there. That was something I never expected.

As the next class arrived, Otto and I drifted together over by the jacket pegs.

"I saw you move in last week," he said.

"You did?" I exclaimed. "Do you live in the big grey house across the street? The one with the white curtains?"

He nodded.

"Then I saw you, too! I wondered who you were."

"Would you like to come over some time?"

"That would be great."

Next, I went to meet Mom at the library. She was waiting in the biography room, the one with the leather wing chairs and the big globe that spins around quite fast—though nothing like as fast as the planet actually spins, of course. She was reading a history of Sundog, and she must have a sixth sense, because when I got within ten steps of her she looked up and smiled. Now, I didn't make any noise or cast a shadow on her page and I don't think that she could smell me at that range. How does she do it? Mothers must have a special kind of kid radar.

"Did you like it?"

"Yes! And guess what? One of the kids in the class —his name is Otto—lives right across the street from us! His big sister does, too. Her name is Zinny."

"In the grey house?"

"That's it."

"Oh, then I met their mom on the stairs. She seems very pleasant. She said her name is Brigid."

"Mom, Otto asked if I could come over sometime. I would really like to."

"That sounds fine. Shall I call Brigid?"

"Just as soon as we get home, please."

We left the library, walked up the hill together, and entered the house that was starting to feel like home.

Laura was right. After just a few lessons, I was able to do a respectable jig. I felt ready for St. Patrick's Day. It was fun walking down the middle of the streets, dancing at certain corners when the music from Laura's boom box cued us. I got to carry the green and white shamrock flag in front most of the time, but twice along the six-block route I handed the flag to Laura and joined with Otto for the reel. Since we were exactly the same height, it was easy to match steps with him.

After the parade, Otto's mom invited us all over to their house. Since she is from Ireland, St. Patrick's Day is a *big* deal for her. She says it wasn't such a big deal when she lived there, but now that she is away from Ireland she celebrates it every way she can. She made us all corned beef and cabbage, and there were fluffy cupcakes with white frosting for dessert. We each got to use a cardboard stencil and sprinkle green sugar on the white frosting, so that we made shamrock cupcakes. Finally, Otto's dad, Vernon, read the story of St. Patrick driving the snakes out of the Emerald Isle. Vernon is tall with dark, dark skin and a moustache. He is from Louisiana originally, so his voice has a beautiful lilt to it, not Irish at all, but foreign-sounding to me. His voice made me think of swamps with alligators and hot sun and honey. Plus, he is a herpetologist—a snake expert—

and teaches biology at Birchwood College, so he knows all about reptiles.

By the first day of spring, it felt as if I had known Otto for years. From then on, we visited each other at least twice a week. He gave me one of his walkie-talkies —it has a range of five miles—and we could talk a little every day at 4:00 p.m. I liked to hide under the bed and pretend we were surrounded by enemies. We invented some code words. I could see the window of his room from my window, and we also used window clings to signal secret messages. A sun meant "Have a nice day!" An American flag meant "Will I see you today?" A leprechaun meant "Yes!" But an Easter egg meant "I have to do my homework—zero chance of playing today." Because Otto was in regular school, we had to plan around his schedule more than around mine.

On the vernal equinox, that day in March when the night and day are exactly the same length, just like they always are at the equator, I was a bit bored. We had been in Sundog for exactly one month. Our house had stopped feeling strange. The quiet of the town was more familiar. And the weather had become decidedly warmer. Most of the snow was gone, and the sidewalks were dry and the breeze was pleasant. Spring was in the air, even if the ground was muddy, the flower beds inactive, and the sky grey as concrete.

I felt restless and cooped up. Mom needed to work on one of her deadlines. The good news was that the publisher liked her cover and had decided to hire her to create a line drawing for each chapter. The not-so-great part was that this meant that she had only two weeks to complete thirteen drawings. I was glad for her, but I felt lonely. There just wasn't anyone to talk to for most of the day, and I was tired of books, DVDs, music, workbooks, and all the inside solo plans I could think of. Finally, Mom said to go outside and get some fresh air.

An old aunt of Dad's, Auntie Margie, had sent us a care package when she heard we were going to be living in a small town. It contained things she had liked to play with as a girl. I had never used any of them in the city: a jump rope, jacks and a ball, and sidewalk chalk, all packed in a pretty bike basket with flowers on it. I didn't have a bike—yet. To tell you the truth, I didn't know how to ride a bike. I was a little afraid of learning.

Anyway, that chalk got me thinking. Did you ever see the movie of Mary Poppins? I know it is a kid movie, but I have always liked it. My favorite character is Bert. He can do just about anything, and he always has a smile on his face, too. My favorite scene is the one where he has made beautiful chalk drawings. His turn out to be magic, and everyone falls into them like Alice down the rabbit hole and then the regular film becomes all mixed up with animation. I don't like that part as much as the beginning of the scene, where Bert is so happy, looking up from his row of pictures with as much pleasure as Mom did when she had just hung a show at a gallery in Chelsea. I love Bert's fruit bowl, especially.

I started in on the rectangle of concrete at the base of our front steps. Not bad. The pinky-red sail boat was pointing straight to Otto's house. I drew a golden frame around it and moved to the next square. I guess I lost track of time, because before I knew it I was at the T intersection where the front walk joined the main sidewalk. When I looked to my left, I had a line of six framed pictures, all different. They looked a little like a string of Tibetan prayer flags or a line of those little nautical flags that dance down from the top of a sailboat mast to the deck.

I was admiring them, but I also wished that I could rotate them 90 degrees so that they were oriented correctly for viewing from the house. Then I realized that no matter how they were oriented, anyone who was approaching the front door would have no choice except to walk right over them. My hands and the knees of my pants were dusted with a dozen colors. Now I was trying to decide whether to turn left or right, or alternate (first left, then right), or just stop and have a snack. I did what I always do when I am mulling over something tough; I rested my right cheek in my right hand and held my right elbow with my left hand. I hummed a little.

"Hello. Are you related to Marc Chagall?" A lady had come up on me from the right and startled me a little. She wore red rain boots, a colorful woolen sweater with big silver buttons, and she wore the white hair on the top of her head in a soft bun. As I stood, I realized that she was only an inch or so taller than I was.

I was flattered to think she found my work anything like the amazing paintings of Marc Chagall.

Have you ever seen them? His work makes me think of dreams and nursery rhymes because of the way he combines people and animals flying like ribbons through colorful landscapes.

"Ummm. No, I'm not a Chagall. I am a Stevens. My mom is an artist, though."

"So are you, I see."

"I guess so." I stuck out my hand, but then looked at it and grinned. "I'm Alexa. Guess you wouldn't want to shake this, though."

"Well, they say it's lucky to shake a chimney sweep's hand, but I have never been lucky enough to meet one. Maybe your artistic talent will rub off on me."

I grinned. The old lady shook my hand warmly.

"I am Viola Davenport," she said. "I live across the street and around that corner. The tall yellow house with the white shutters. Lived here for nearly forty years. I taught classics at Birchwood, Greek and Latin. My husband is of English birth, yet he teaches Norwegian. My own people are from Norway. I was born a Svenson."

"Is your sweater from Norway?"

"It is, indeed. Well, Alexa, do you know how to draw anything Norwegian?"

Mrs. Davenport spoke excellent English, but I could hear the lingering echoes of a Scandinavian childhood in the way it sounded like she was saying, "Vell, Alexa," and, "Norvegian."

I thought for a moment. "How about a Viking ship?"

"Splendid! You draw a longship pointed that way, to my house. I shall do as all proper patrons do, and reward you with the coin of the realm. Here you go!"

Mrs. Davenport reached under her sweater into the pocket of her trousers. Then she laid two quarters and three pennies into my palm. They looked very nice there on the smudgy backdrop of chalk colors. "That's the change from my morning coffee," she said.

"It's a deal!" I said. And I began outlining the ship and drawing around the quarters to make a row of shields.

"I will wander by later to see the result. Welcome to the neighborhood, Alexa."

I waved and bent over the new drawing, planning a bright blue sea and a red and white striped sail, and a row of bronze shields keeping watch over the oars. I could hardly believe my luck! I just bet that Mrs. Davenport would be the kind of person to enjoy Norse myths. I was pretty sure that I had made another friend.

Chapter Three
"Zorro and the Leprechaun"

April in Minnesota is a magical month. Overnight, the grass transforms—Presto! Chango!—from dull brown to a lush, vibrant green that almost hurts the eyes. I remember that first April really well. First, because I remember everything. And second, because it was when Mom and I started going to the homeschool play group at the Sundog Public Library. That is where I met two new kids who looked interesting.

When I walked in the door I saw a tall, skinny, friendly-looking boy. He was too far away for me to hear what he was saying, but the other two boys near him were laughing at something he said. When I drifted over, he gave me a smile. Then he said to us all, "Want to see a magic trick?"

"Sure!" we all replied.

One of the little boys next to me said, "Ed is the best. Just watch."

The tall boy shuffled a deck of cards deftly, then fanned it out on a table. "Go ahead," he said to me. "Pick any card. Don't show it to me, but you can show it to them if you like."

I drew out the six of hearts, flashed it to the other two boys, and looked questioningly at Ed, who had shaped the remaining cards back into a deck.

"Return your card to the deck," he instructed, cutting the deck open to receive my randomly drawn card. "Now I will shuffle and cut a few times." His thin fingers managed to make the deck appear to be a waterfall or a living thing. Then he placed the deck on the table and covered it with a white silk handkerchief.

"Knock and ask," he gestured to me, "for your friend to open the door. Call her by name."

I lightly tapped on the smooth and slippery mound with my knuckles and, feeling a bit silly, said, "Open the door, Six of Hearts."

The magician boy (that is what I was calling him to myself) picked up a corner of the handkerchief and whisked it away. Then he said to me, "Your friend can't hear you. Knock and call again."

Then I really felt goony, but I did it.

"She is behind the door, but you must help her to open it," and he gestured to me.

I turned over the top card. It was the six of hearts! I actually felt my jaw drop. "How did you do that?"

He smiled, while the others shifted and clapped. "Magic, *naturalmente*."

Then the little boys were called by their mother. They were brothers called Scot and Sandy, and it was time for their haircuts so they had to leave. I turned to the magician boy.

"So, your name is Ed?"

"Well, Eduardo, actually. Eduardo Suarez, at your service." He put his hand on his heart and clicked his heels together and bowed. I kid you not. I couldn't help but giggle.

"But you can call me Ed. Lots of people do."

Eduardo was tall, with a thin face and medium brown hair. He had green eyes. In a few moments, I felt like I had known him forever. He liked action figures, doing magic tricks, and telling jokes. He was born in Barcelona and had moved to Sundog two years ago, but he didn't have a Spanish accent. His mother did, though, and so did his father, I found out later.

As Ed was putting away his cards, a girl walked in through the door with her mother. "Hey there, Leprechaun!" he called.

The mother, who was shaking a big, wet umbrella, smiled, while the girl held a cardboard box to one side so it wouldn't get wet. The box looked as though it had been wrapped in a map. The girl was tiny. I wondered who she was. Although she didn't smile, she didn't seem afraid or particularly unfriendly.

She walked over to us and said, "Hi, Zorro! I have a new puzzle. Would you like to help me put it together?"

"Let's see it, Isabelle," he said.

Isabelle showed us both a jigsaw puzzle of the world. It had 500 pieces, with a little tiny flag on each country.

"That looks like fun," I said.

"You can help, too," said Isabelle.

We sat around one of the tables. I learned that Isabelle Porter and Eduardo Suarez were the same age as me, nearly ten, but she only came up to about my ear lobe, while he was two inches taller than I am. She was called Leprechaun because of her size and her golden hair but she wasn't Irish at all. Isabelle had a cloud of fine blonde hair and blue eyes. Her chin was pointed so her face was shaped like a heart. She wore round, steel-colored glasses that she called "specs." She didn't say much, but she was very quick at sorting the puzzle pieces. Eduardo said that Isabelle is really good at doing anything with her hands—painting, drawing, cooking, and just making things like sculptures from bits of this and that. She is good at growing things, too. She even knows sign language. She seemed very serious at first, because she doesn't talk nearly as much as I do. In fact, she seemed a little bit shy. But she had a bright smile once she was comfortable enough to show it. She told me that her mom, who was a doctor, helped her make models of the heart and the lungs out of clay but that her dad did most of the homeschool teaching at their house. Also, she had two pesty twin brothers but she wished she had a sister. And she was a good listener, even before we were friends. Now she is the first person I want to tell when I have a secret.

We were making lots of progress on assembling the puzzle. We had most of the border complete, about half of the western hemisphere, almost all of Europe, and piles of Asia and Africa.

"Where do you live?" asked Isabelle.

"We just moved to Cherryvale Street," I answered.

"Do you know Otto Bell?"

"You bet! He's in my dance class. We were in the St. Patrick's Day parade together. He's great. But I wish he wasn't in school all day."

"I know," said Eduardo. "Do you ever wonder what it is like to go into a school and stay there all day?"

"I did that in kindergarten," I said. "For part of first grade, too."

"Do you miss it?" Isabelle rested her chin on her hand and looked at me. Her eyes looked very blue and big through her lenses.

I thought a moment. "Some parts," I said.

"All the kids in books go to school," she said, "unless they are on desert islands."

"Right," Eduardo agreed. "Even the ones set in other times or where the kids are magic or on vacation. School is always there around the corner."

"But there are more than two million homeschool kids in the U.S. now," I said. "How come no one has written a book about us?"

"Somebody will, someday," said Isabelle with a firm nod.

"Maybe it will be a movie!" I said. "Hey, guys! Does anyone have a video camera?"

They both shook their heads. My shoulders sagged. "Well…" I was about to say that maybe we could write the book ourselves, but then Mom came over and I needed to introduce her to my new friends. Then it was time to go, which made me feel even more droopy, until Mom said that we could come back to the group every week.

As we left, I realized that my Sundog Kid-Friend Portfolio had increased by 200 percent that afternoon. I now had three great pals, plus Mrs. Davenport. I felt very wealthy indeed.

Chapter Four
"Wild Bear"

When the weather got warmer, Eduardo, Isabelle, Otto, and I decided to go on an adventure. It was a Saturday. They told me they were going to take me to a special wild secret place where there were snakes, fish, raccoons, and even deer. Isabelle told me that once she had been walking there with her mother and they had seen a fawn, lying in the grass, all alone. I guessed that a fawn would feel perfectly comfortable with Isabelle, because she was so quiet and still herself.

Me, I like to whistle back at the song birds, caw at the crows, meow at the cats, and say "Here, good boy" to all the dogs. For some reason, I think of every dog as a boy and every cat as a girl, even though I know that isn't true. I also like to laugh and sing and talk and crash through the grass. I think my chances of observing a fawn are remote.

Otto's mom, Brigid, had said that she would pack us lunches, so we could spend all morning and afternoon in the Birchwood Arboretum if we liked. I believe in troubleshooting, so I put some extra supplies in my stripy backpack: sunglasses, bug spray, a disposable camera, a magnifying glass, disinfectant, bandages, cookies (in case there wasn't enough dessert for everyone), a bottle of water, a mechanical pencil (doesn't need sharpening), a blank note book, and a joke book. I wore my new sneakers with the hot pink laces and a green denim cap. Mom insisted that I put on lots of sun block. I hate the smell and feel of it, but our many discussions of the pain of sunburn, the acceleration of wrinkles, and the increased odds of skin cancer keep me quiet. It's true that my backpack was a little heavy, but I like to be prepared.

As I climbed the steps to Otto's porch, I could see that the others were almost ready.

"Come in, come in," said Brigid in a voice like song. To me, everything she says sounds like music. I would love to visit Ireland sometime. "I've got the lunches readied," she continued. "Well, love," she paused and held me at arm's length looking me and my backpack up and down, a slow smile curving on her face. "You look ready for anything at all."

"I've never been a Girl Scout, but I don't like to be caught short," I said.

"I see that. I do. Well, no rubbing sticks to make sparks and that, okay?"

Otto giggled. Isabelle smiled. Eduardo adjusted his hat.

She handed each of us a nice fat brown paper bag. "Here are all the goods: sandwiches, the obligatory carrot sticks, some sliced pears, and... cupcakes!"

"Yum," I said reaching for mine. "Thanks!"

I was just able to squeeze the sack into the top of my backpack. It was good to know that it would be a good deal lighter on the way home, unless I found lots of interesting specimens.

We poured out of the house and ran all the way to the corner. Saturdays in spring are very beautiful. The air was soft and smelled sweet because the grass was greening up. Some of the trees even had leaf buds, and I spotted lots of late crocus and some daffodils in neighbor gardens. Our garden had no flowers at all, just a few limp shrubs, grass, and river stones over black paper around the house. Dad and Mom were planning to change that. They had been watching how the sun falls to find where things like to grow. Dad has a lot of confidence as a gardener. For Mom it was all new. I was excited to think about planting a garden all my own, even making a house out of sunflowers with a morning glory roof. We had some seeds started inside, but since it was too early to put them outside, I had contented myself with drawing flowers with sidewalk chalk on the foundation blocks. They looked very nice, and because no one walked on them, they lasted a long time.

"So," I asked. "Where are we going?"

"This way!" said Otto. We crossed over Montgomery Street and stepped onto the Birchwood campus. I could see the sun striking off the gothic windows of the red brick dormitories. Then, as we headed down the hill, we saw the sparkling blue of Teagarden Lake, the tiny artificial widening of Spring Creek where it flows artistically under three bridges and around two man-made islands before spilling into the culvert under Highway 3 and west into the Bucklehorn River.

My backpack was beginning to feel heavy, but I didn't want to complain. Also, I was thinking about that cupcake from Brigid, even though I had just finished breakfast.

"So," I said. "Are we heading to one of the islands?" The islands were neat. I had been to both of them before, and I really liked the one with the labyrinth set into the grass with paving stones. Unfortunately the wild geese that frequented the island liked it, too, so sometimes it was slick with goose poop. But it was a pretty island with a picnic table. The other kids might think I hadn't been there, so I could play along, pretend it was a new adventure.

Eduardo looked at me sideways and smiled mysteriously.

"No?" I caught Isabelle's eye.

"Nope," said Isabelle as she adjusted her cap brim lower, so I couldn't see her blue eyes dancing. She wanted to tell me, but she wouldn't. Already I knew her well enough to know that nothing would induce her to talk until she was ready.

"Otto, come on, I am dying here. I have got to know." I exaggerated, but I was quite curious.

Otto smiled his infectious smile, shrugged his shoulders, and started to hum.

Clearly it was a conspiracy. No one was going to cough up even a little clue. I saw that I might as well stop asking and enjoy the mystery of it all.

We wound our way through a path in the prairie restoration project, past the bur oak, and around a stand of trees. Then the path curved along the edge of Spring Creek, and we followed it upstream for about ten minutes. No one else was around. The trees—linden, maple, birch—were growing so closely together it was like being in a woven tunnel until the path came to an opening. There a wide bridge, a large grey curve of concrete like a child's block, spanned the creek.

Eduardo led the way through some bushes down the bank of the creek. It was muddy, but we moved carefully along the fast-running water to some natural stepping stones. These seven stones were rounded and mossy, just large enough to balance on. They led to a small island, a sandbar, really, but covered with new green grass, that lay right in the middle of Spring Creek. We stepped onto the sunny west end, grateful to feel solid earth again after a few seconds of slippery footing. The island was about three paces wide and about ten paces long. The far end was sunk into the shadows under the bridge, pointing east.

"This is…" I was about to say "Great!" but before I could, Otto shushed me.

We all crouched down and looked where he pointed.

A short way upstream, on top of a huge boulder that looked like a plaything for Paul Bunyan, stood a child. She had long blondish-brown hair pulled back in a braid. She wore a white undershirt and muddy-looking denim shorts. Her toes curved over the mossy edge of the granite ledge. There were stripes of mud on her cheeks and swirls of mud on her arms. Most startling of all was how she stood: completely still. Her right arm was upraised, holding a long pointed stick. She was looking intently into the water, but not like Narcissus. She was too fierce for that. Rather, she looked like a muscular fairy, or maybe one of Peter Pan's Lost Boys.

"Who is that?" I asked in a quiet voice. I didn't want to startle her.

"Don't know," said Eduardo, equally quietly.

Isabelle shrugged and shook her head.

"I think she goes to Sibley. She doesn't go to Rachel Carson Elementary with us, but I think I saw her at the all-school picnic," whispered Otto.

As we watched, the girl made a movement so swift it didn't register at first. Then, we saw the spear break through the sparkling water. A second later, the girl shouted, "Rats! Missed again."

"What are you doing?" I called.

The girl replied, "Not fishing, I guess," and kept her gaze locked onto the water. Then she turned toward us and said, "Hey! Grab my spear!"

Isabelle shucked off her sneakers and stepped lightly out into the shallows of the stream just as the long stick floated by. She grasped it firmly and pulled it out of the water, backing up onto the little shoal.

Meanwhile, the strange girl had scrambled down from her granite perch and was approaching along the south bank. She climbed up, appeared for a moment at the end of the bridge, and then half-jogged, half-slid down the other side. Scorning the stepping stones, she strode sure-footedly into the swift-running stream. Before I knew it, she was standing before us, dripping like a wet dog, holding out her hand.

"Hi," I grasped her outstretched hand. "I'm Alexa."

When I felt an electric jump of surprise in the girl's hand, I mentally kicked myself, remembering not every child in Minnesota shook hands the way I had been taught to do. She must have been reaching for her spear. "Um," I said, trying to put her at ease. "Would you like a cupcake?"

That made her smile. She nodded, and sank lightly into a cross-legged position. Isabelle handed her the spear. The girl patted it and positioned it within easy reach.

"I'm Otto," said Otto. "Do you go to Sibley?"

The girl nodded. "You don't," she stated. "None of you do."

"That's right," said Eduardo. "Isabelle, Alexa, and I are all homeschooled.

Otto spoke again. "I go to Rachel Carson. So did my sister, Zinny. Now she's at the middle school."

I had undone my backpack straps and was unwrapping the waxed paper from the cupcake. The butter-cream frosting had smashed a little, but otherwise it was in good shape. I offered it to the girl and she took it.

"Thanks," she said. Then she added, "I'm Ursula Donaldson."

The other kids took out their lunches, too, and pretty soon we were all laughing and talking. Ursula told us that she had recently read a great book about a girl who lives all alone, called *Island of the Blue Dolphins*. The main character had to find all her own food, and had learned to fish with a spear that she had made herself. Ursula had wanted to test out her own ability to survive.

"Did you have any luck?" asked Otto.

"I certainly hope not," said Isabelle.

"When you hold the spear, do you lay the shaft across your wrist?" wondered Eduardo.

"My favorite book about a girl surviving on her own is called *Julie of the Wolves*. Have you read it?" I asked.

Ursula answered all our questions: she hadn't had any luck, but she had enjoyed making the spear and watching for fish. The shadows under the surface of the water were beautiful, but she had built up a ravenous hunger and was very glad for a cupcake with frosting. She would have to toughen up if she were going to make it in the wild. She didn't lay her spear along her wrist, but it sounded worth trying, and Eduardo was welcome to test out the various throwing options. She hadn't read *Julie of the Wolves* yet, but she had heard it was good.

It turned out that Ursula lived with her dad on the other side of the river, near Isabelle's house. Her dad wasn't going to be home until dinner time, and so she was free to do whatever she wanted to do until then. She showed us the house key on a leather thong around her neck.

"See," she said, proudly. "As long as I am careful to lock up, I can go anywhere I can ride my bike."

None of us said anything. None of us had ever even dreamed of that kind of freedom. It was a little bit scary, but we envied her, too.

"What if you need help?" asked Isabelle.

"I never do," said Ursula. "But, if I did, I could go over to the Campbell house on the corner. Mrs. Campbell is always there. She has twins who are only three and a new baby, too. Sometimes I go there for lunch. I help the little guys eat, and she makes me a sandwich."

I felt better about that. At least she wasn't completely alone.

After we finished eating, we spent a little time tossing the spear and looking for long sticks so we could make our own. We watched the tadpoles flit across the dappled shallows, scattering without injury as soon as the shadow of an arm or spear crossed their vision.

Since Ursula didn't have to be home until the evening, she agreed to come back to Otto's house with us. We hid the spears in the woods, then hiked up to where Ursula had parked her bike, affectionately named "Rusty Red," and then we all walked through the campus back to Otto's house.

Brigid welcomed us, but didn't interrupt her gardening. She told us that there were cold drinks in the fridge, snacks in the cupboard, and, pointedly, that there was no shortage of soap and fresh towels in the downstairs bathrooms.

"Your mom is nice," said Ursula to Otto.

"Yeah? I guess so."

After we ate, we got out a fun board game that combined trivia questions with charades. We laughed until our sides ached. My dad was mowing our lawn across the street, and he stopped by to say that he could hear our shrieks and giggles over the roar of the machine.

We had so much fun that, before Ursula rode off on Rusty Red and Mrs. Suarez collected Eduardo and Isabelle, we all agreed to meet at Otto's house the next Saturday and do it all again.

When the next Saturday came, the clouds were like black and grey whales swimming through the sky. All the mothers shook their heads at the idea of a picnic hike. Then Ursula came riding up on Rusty Red just as a gust sent some drops of rain onto the porch, driving us inside.

"Rats," said Otto. "This is crummy weather. I really wanted a picnic."

"Anyone want to play a board game?" I asked half-heartedly.

Brigid popped her head into the dining room, where all five of us were slumped on chairs. "Hello, all," she said. "Why such glum looks, eh?"

"Rain," we all sighed together.

She laughed in a pleasant way, twitching the lace curtain aside. "I don't call that rain," she said. "I call it 'cookie-baking weather.'"

"Hurray!" we all cried.

An hour later, we all felt much better. The kitchen was filled with the comforting smells of sugar, peanut butter, and chocolate, and our stomachs were comfortably full of warm samples of our handiwork.

"Thank you, Brigid," Isabelle said.

"There is always a silver lining, my gram used to say," Brigid responded. "You lot did me an enormous favor. I had volunteered to provide six dozen cookies for the Garden Club bake sale on Monday, and I wasn't sure when I could fit it in. Now, my work is done." She smiled at us all, and the deep dimple on the left side of her face flashed on the surface. Then she picked up a chocolate chip cookie, all gooey with melted chips and took a bite. "Mmmmmm."

"Say," Brigid continued. "It looks like the rain is letting up."

It was true. A bit of sunlight bounced onto the dining room table as if on cue.

"Yeah, but it is too wet for the island," I groused. Maybe it was the city girl in me, but I just hate sitting on wet grass. I hoped the others didn't insist on it.

"Would you children consider doing me another favor?" mused Brigid.

"What is it? Baking cakes?" asked Isabelle.

"No. See that huge stack of library books?" Brigid pointed to the table near the door. It was piled high with books, many of them thick coffee-table books on the history of dance and the geography of Russia. "I gave my paper on Anna Pavlova to my book group on Thursday," she said.

Otto sprang up onto the toes of his red high-topped sneakers and pirouetted, then sank to his knees, fluttering his extended arms a little, then came to stillness. It was a very credible imitation of the Dying Swan, at least until he lifted his head. Then his black eyes sparkled and his grin lit up his face and we all just had to laugh. Pathos was not Otto's strong point.

"Very nice, boyo," said Brigid. "I've been meaning to return these, but they are so heavy that it is just too much for one trip. But if you divide this stack by five... yes! Just two books apiece. The library is such a fine place to spend a wet afternoon, and you could check out a DVD to bring home to watch."

"That's a great idea!" said Otto, looking around to make sure we all agreed. We did.

Each of us hoisted up two of the massive books and headed single-file down the sidewalk. We must have looked like a parade of librarians or maybe a book worm inching along: Isabelle as the head, Eduardo, me and Ursula as the midsections, and Otto as the tail. The Sundog Public Library was three blocks away. Somehow —I think Eduardo started it—we began singing the changing of the guard song, from the Wicked Witch of the West's castle stronghold in *The Wizard of Oz*. You know how it goes: "Oh wee oh, Oh No!" We sang it over and over, in a very low register. Our steps synchronized with the chant automatically. (Actually, to me, the sound changed to "moNEo, MOne" two forms of the second conjugation Latin verb, monere, which, fittingly, means "to warn." But I could tell I shouldn't interrupt the parade to tell my friends that.) We marched in place at the street corners until the traffic cleared, not stopping until we reached the library plaza.

The rain had left the tulips in the planter sparkling with dew. The grass must have been mowed the day before, because it was short, lush, green, and smelled heavenly. A robin sang in the bough of the mock orange bush. Its breast was exactly the color of the brick wall. As soon as its song ended, the bells of St. John's church across the river began to ring, even though it wasn't Sunday or anything. It was a moment of pure quiet beauty that I wanted to put in my pocket and keep forever.

But, since I couldn't, I said, "Last one to the circulation desk is a rotten archaeopteryx egg!" Then I bolted for the entrance.

Inside, we all slowed to a halt when we saw Ms. Rachel, the library director. She was really nice, but somehow we all knew that she frowned on running inside the building. We each, in turn, thumped the books we carried on the counter, then gravitated to the wall where the DVDs were shelved.

Ms. Rachel walked toward us, a big smile under her big glasses. Her white hair was piled high on her head. She was as skinny as an exclamation point and walked with just a bit of a limp under her long, flowered skirt.

"Just the people I was hoping to see," she said.

"Who, us?" I asked.

"Yes, Alexa. I need all of you to consider helping me out."

"What's the problem, Ms. Rachel?" Eduardo asked.

"Our summer reading program for the young readers kicks off in two weeks," she began.

"I know," Ursula interrupted. "I signed up to be a junior activity coordinator."

"We are depending on that, Ursula," Ms. Rachel continued. "But there's a problem that I just learned we have." She waved a page of printed e-mail correspondence limply, as though it were a white flag of surrender. I wasn't used to seeing Ms. Rachel discouraged.

"What's that?" Isabelle asked.

"I am afraid that our kick-off event has cancelled."

"Austen Phillips isn't coming?" Otto said what we were all thinking. We'd all been looking forward to the concert with this singer of great kid songs. Sure, maybe we were too old to go, but every one of us had some of his CDs, and the songs were catchy, and well, lovable. I know I had hoped to have him autograph the picture of him that came with my copy of his CD called "Catfish Fever and Other Humdingers."

"Rats!" said Ursula. Her face was all red. I was a little afraid she might kick something.

"It is disappointing," agreed Ms. Rachel. "But there might be a silver lining here."

We waited. That silver lining was flipping all over the place today like a trout in a fast brook.

"We've got to have some music... what about our local groups?" she continued.

Otto broke in, "That's true, but it's not the same kind of show. I mean, Austen Phillips has some razzle-dazzle, some showmanship."

"True," said Ms. Rachel. "But so does Eduardo."

Eduardo blushed a little and raised his eyebrows, then gazed quizzically over Ms. Rachel's shoulder.

"You want Eduardo to do some magic?" I asked. I remembered the first time I had seen him doing card tricks here at the library. He really *was* good. But a whole show?

"Well, this is just an idea. But when I saw Eddie, I thought of all the talent in this town. I started to wonder about having a talent showcase for some of the great bands and singers. What I thought was that Eddie could be the master of ceremonies and also, if he wanted to, do a few magic tricks. Maybe some of you could assist?"

Ms. Rachel looked so hopeful that I hoped Eduardo would say yes.

"Yes!" said Eduardo. "My Uncle Geraldo sent me some new tricks last week. I haven't shown anyone in town yet."

"And you have that wonderful swirly cape," Otto said.

"Hey, do you want to cut me in half?" asked Ursula. "I'm not afraid."

"You'll be wonderful, Zorro," said Isabelle. "I can help with the props."

We forgot all about the DVDs. For the next half hour, we adjourned to the conference table in Ms. Rachel's office and chattered about props, like feathered hoops and silk scarves, as well as who would get to help

Eduardo with each act. Eduardo didn't seem nervous at all, but, as I walked home, I thought about how I can be kind of klutzy, and I got a lump in my throat. I just wanted to help. *What if I wrecked everything instead?*

Chapter Five
"On with the Show"

A week later, the program was all set. Three great bands would appear and donate their time, so the Austen Phillips fee would be able to buy books for the library instead. All of us—even Isabelle—were a little stage-struck, but we had worked it out so that we all got a turn. Each of us would get to help Eduardo with one trick. He was very excited, too. Together with Ms. Rachel, he worked out a stage name for himself, a name for the show, and a few words of introduction for each act. After I told him I'd lend him my joke books, he thought he would incorporate a few jokes, too. We all agreed: it was going to be a wonderful show.

June 13th dawned clear and warm. By noon, the local Showmobile, Sundog's portable stage, was in place at Bridge Square near the river. At 3:00 p.m., we were all in place in our stage finery for sound checks. Ursula's dad, Mike Donaldson, who was a sound and lights expert—and sometimes an actor—at the Guthrie Theater in Minneapolis, was there, too. It was the first time any of us (except Ursula, of course) had met him.

He had offered to come and give us some stage make-up so our faces could be seen from across the square.

"Hi, Mr. Donaldson," I said as I walked over. "Do you need any help?"

"Hi. You must be Alexa," he answered, not looking away from his handiwork on Isabelle. She looked great, actually, from a distance, but up close she looked like a painted doll. I guess that is the point—in reverse, since the idea was to make her look vivid from far away. "No," he said. "I think I am all set. I will be ready to do your makeup in five minutes. Oh, and can the 'Mr.,' okay? Just call me Mike."

"Okay," I said, and left them to check on everyone else.

Eduardo was behind the stage warming up his fingers for the sleight-of-hand business he had planned. He was wearing his silk top hat from his Uncle Geraldo and looking down at his sleeve.

I went over to him and tapped him on the shoulder. "Hey."

He looked up and smiled.

I was so surprised I started to laugh. "Wow! I've never seen you with black eyebrows or lipstick," I said.

Eduardo grinned. "Mike wanted to paint on a mustache. With curled ends, no less. But that would be too villainous for me."

"I'll say."

"What about you? Do you have stage fright? Shall we go with Plan B? I can always saw you in half. Shouldn't be that hard."

"Very funny. I am not nervous a bit. Well, maybe a bit. I don't want to drop anything."

"Uncle Geraldo's wife, Tia Bianca, is a dancer. Do you know what she says?"
I shook my head.

"Just keep smiling and moving your feet, and no one will know if you miss a step. So if you do drop something, just do a pretend 'Oops!' all exaggerated, and everyone will think we planned it for comic relief."

"Hey! There are your parents." I pointed.

Victor and Constanza Suarez walked leisurely through the crowd. Perhaps it would be more accurate to say that the crowd parted in front of them. Even in New York, this couple would have been noticed. Both were tall—over six feet—slim, and well dressed. They moved gracefully, Mrs. Suarez in a sleeveless black dress and a lilac shawl, Mr. Suarez in cream-colored linen trousers and a loose cut burgundy shirt.

Somehow, seeing the elegance of Eduardo's parents made me nervous. They had traveled the world. They would probably expect a lot. Maybe that was why Zorro was nervous, too. Well, I would just do the best I could. It was too bad that my part didn't come until right before the second band. But for now, I was just going to try to enjoy the music.

My parents were sitting in the middle on the aisle. I saw them talking to Brigid and Vernon Bell. Mrs. Davenport and Mr. Davenport were in the center of the row. Mrs. Davenport wore a big straw hat and long loose sleeves. I knew that she was very susceptible to mosquito bites, and that the net scarf wound around the hat brim could be let down, like a bee keeper's veil, if they became too vicious. Ms. Rachel was checking in here and there, making certain that everything was running smoothly. Then I saw Laura Hogan, our Irish step dance teacher, over by the fountain. As usual, she had a flock of little five- and six-year-olds following her, trying to imitate the fancy footwork she was demonstrating. She looked up, waved and smiled, and sank gracefully down to the grass to watch the show.

Otto and Isabelle walked over, all made up. "It's your turn," said Isabelle. "Hurry!"

I hustled over to the makeup table. Mike's brushes tickled just a little as he outlined my eyes, painted my lips, and gave me rouge spots on each cheek.

I looked in the mirror and said, "Cool. Thanks!" before I returned to the waiting area behind the stage. "Where's Ursula?" I asked Eduardo as we stood waiting for the show to start.

"She'll be right back," he said.

There was a blare of recorded trumpets, and Eduardo said, "That means I have 60 seconds. Here goes nothing!"

I gave him the thumbs up sign and a big smile. Then I walked around to the side by the front of the show mobile so I could watch. Eduardo mounted the steps and stepped from the wings onto the center of the stage. He paused, just for a moment, and I held my breath. *Please, please, let him do well*, I thought just as hard as I could.

Then Eddie smiled his great big smile, held out his cape with his right hand, tipped his silk top hat with his left and bowed deeply. "Ladies and gentleman! Thank you! I am your host, Zorro Zoliath. Welcome to the Sundog Summer Bash for Books!"

The applause was strong, and the show had begun.

Ursula flew in at the last minute, dropped Rusty Red, and moved into position. Her makeup was in place, so her dad must have done her first, at home.

Zinny sauntered into the group. She gave Otto the high five and me the low five and winked at Isabelle, whose eyes looked huge behind her specs. "Don't worry, guys. You'll do great! And afterwards, we're all going out for ice cream."

Then I realized I was nervous because the mention of ice cream might as well have been the promise of a dish of sawdust.

Zinny gave us all an encouraging smile and went to join the audience.

The introductions ended, and the first band started up. It was called "Bonnie and the Clydes," a favorite local group who sang songs from the 1960s and 1970s. Bonnie and the Clydes had wonderful harmonies, a little like Peter, Paul, and Mary. I was glad the most soothing of the bands was on first. If they had started with Jeanie and the Punkatronics, I probably would have jumped out of my skin.

Bonnie and the Clydes played for about half an hour. Then it was time for Eduardo again. We planned that he would do a couple of jokes and then I would assist him with a magic trick before the middle band, Wonder Bread, came on.

Everything was going well. Eduardo was a natural, and his nervousness seemed to have vanished completely. I was glad he was confident. Now he was telling a joke: "What did Zero say to Eight? Nice belt!"

There it was! The punch line was my cue.

My heart pounded and my mouth grew dry. For one eerie, terrifying moment, I just plain froze. Then, sucking in as full a breath as I could manage, I stepped out of the shadows and onto the stage.

"Ladies and gentleman," Eduardo called out, "I give you the Amazing Alexa. She will assist me in a most wondrous trick, previously known to only the shamans of a remote tribe up the Amazon."

I knew my part was to take the three feathered hoops from Eduardo and to test them for breaks, then hand them back with a flourish. Simple enough, right? Well, not so simple for me, apparently. I took the hoops, but I pulled on them so hard that one flew out of my hands and into the audience. It bounced on the ground, rolled a moment, and lay on the grass.

Everyone gave a big laugh. I was glad for the makeup and general twilight. I could feel the hot prickling blush spread from my heart all the way to the roots of my hair. "Oops!" I said.

Everyone laughed harder as an older gentleman reached down, picked up the hoop and stood. He gave a little extra tug on it, and reached it up to me. I bowed to him and smiled, then returned the hoop to Eduardo.

He quickly transformed the single hoop into three linked hoops and back into one again. With a flourish, he pulled the shining circle over his shoulders, turned it briefly into a hula-hoop, caught it, and neatly stepped out of it. Then he tipped his top hat to the audience, and we were done.

My heart was still racing when I bowed and accompanied Eduardo off the stage, but now I wasn't afraid, just excited. When the worst happens (well, okay, not the worst, but my worst-case scenario) it helps to have a plan. Maybe nothing is as bad in real life as it is in your mind. Mom and Dad were standing up, clapping and cheering. I went over to them and sat down in the empty chair beside Dad.

"Nice job!" Mom mouthed over the opening chords of Wonder Bread's first song. Wonder Bread was the oddest *a cappella* group: Lutheran blonds breaking like fractals into a barbershop quartet, triple trio, and hand bell choir, then reforming seamlessly into a chorus. But it worked.

The rest of the evening passed in a haze of contentment. I got to watch Otto, Ursula, and Isabelle on stage with Eduardo. I think the makeup helped, because even Isabelle was not too shy to speak up and smile. By the time Jeanie and the Punkatronics came on, the stars were out and I was ravenously hungry. I wandered over to the food stands and sampled some of everything: curly fries, mini doughnuts, cheese curds, corn dogs, corn on the cob, and cotton candy. Then it was time to congratulate Eduardo and connect with Mom and Dad so we could all head over for ice cream.

As we left Bridge Square, Ms. Rachel flagged me down and gave me a big hug. That startled me a little, but I liked it. "Alexa!" she said, "you were wonderful in that improvisation. I didn't know you had a gift for comedy."

"Me, either," I admitted.

"Tonight was a triumph," she continued, "for our town and for the library, too. It's a little too early to know for sure, but my guess is that we raised almost $4000 for the book fund." Her big glasses gleamed in the lamplight.

"And you threw a heck of a party," Dad chimed in.

Later, as I drifted off to sleep, applause still ringing in my ears, I smiled. Helen Keller wrote that "Life is either a daring adventure or nothing." It seemed odd to me that in this little town I was growing more daring than I ever had been in the big city. Being on stage was definitely outside of my comfort zone, but then, when you push out of your comfort zone, the whole zone enlarges. Who knew what I would be able to do next? All I knew was that my friends and family would be there to see me do it. I was so happy, I didn't even need to wish on a star or try to name any of them. I just drifted off to sleep with melodies from the last hundred years blowing through my mind like colored silk scarves tumbling in the wind.

Chapter Six
"The Howling Vowels Make a Splash"

N o doubt about it, summertime is great. Despite being named for something freezing cold, Sundog is very fun in the summer. It is *way* more fun than New York City, actually. In Manhattan, there is so much concrete that you feel pretty baked and limp in the summer. Everything outside is too hot to touch. Plus, it smells like dog pee a lot. I know dogs can't use toilets, and they have to go somewhere, but still.

In Sundog, however, there are long green lawns and big shade trees. It is hot here, too, but there are more breezes and open spaces. One of my favorite places is under the bridge at the Birchwood College Arboretum. The bridge goes over the winding curves of Spring Creek. Underneath there is a shallow sandbar you can get to with only two steps in the water. One of the students painted graffiti there, but it's not like you think. It is a rectangle about two by three feet with a thick border. Inside is a picture of white clouds drifting in a blue sky. It looks just like a painting in a museum, except that instead of being hung on a white wall with lots of people going by, it kind of floats in the dark green shadows by the creek. That is one of the coolest places I've found in Sundog.

The other place is a swimming pool. In Sundog there was a new city swimming pool with fountains and lifeguard chairs and changing rooms and even a high diving board. It is just six blocks from my house, so after school let out and it opened for the season, the gang and I would go over every other day or so. It is lots of fun.

My favorite pool, however, is what you might call "semi-private." A wonderful lady named Ann Hanson has a pool in her back garden and she is a very experienced swimming coach, so she gives swimming lessons to kids in the summer. Miss Ann is very encouraging and because her lessons are one-on-one, I never feel worried that I am going to flub up a move. I have to say that I am still not the strongest swimmer, but that first summer in Sundog I did greatly improve with Miss Ann cheering me on. Her garden was very peaceful, and although she had a few other teachers, too, the pool was never crowded or noisy. I just loved it.

My tenth birthday was on July 22nd. After our first 4th of July celebration in Sundog, which we spent on the hill overlooking the river, slapping mosquitoes and ooing and ahhing over fireworks, it was time to plan my birthday party. Mom asked me what I would like to have.

"Cake and ice cream, of course," I said.

"Of course." Mom stood up from the table, went into the kitchen, and came back with a pen and a clipboard. I think I have mentioned that Mom takes the planning process very seriously. You would think that she would be ditzy and dreamy because she is an artist, but she's not. Mom is very creative, but she says things like "A plan is a dream with a deadline" and "What steps do we need to translate this idea into reality?"

The guest list was no problem: Otto, Eduardo, Isabelle, and Ursula.

Mom said, "It is hard to believe that you just met these children. Somehow you've formed a pack."

I nodded thoughtfully and considered the word *pack*. Mom and I had traveled up to the Wolf Center in Ely, Minnesota, way up by Canada, at the end of June. I had never seen so many trees or slapped so many mosquitoes. We learned lots of facts about wolves. I even managed to get one photo of a distant wolf. There were enough pixels to blow it up so that its face was visible, and we had a print of it taped to the window near the back door, facing out, along with a postcard photo of Peter Lorre, that actor from old movies who always played villains. Those were to scare away intruders, we joked. I guess we still had a bit of that big city nervousness about strangers, even though Sundog is so safe that some people don't even lock their doors. Hard to believe, I know.

Anyway, Mom was right about us. My friends and I *were* like a pack of wolves. We were all close to the same age, so no one was a silverback. But we were curious, playful, loyal to each other, and rather self-sufficient. With five of us, there was always someone around to talk to or play games with or just hang out with. I had met some other nice kids in Sundog but I just didn't need any other friends.

"Yep," Mom continued, "a *really vocal* pack."

When Mom gets a metaphor, she doesn't like to let it drop. I knew that she was referring to what we learned about how wolves communicate. The naturalist said that they communicate in three ways: sense of smell, body language, and vocalizations, which include howls, barks, growls, and whimpers.

"I could be more vocal with a cell phone," I said, not-so-subtly hinting. "That would make a terrific birthday gift for a busy parent."

"Nice try, Ace," Mom said. "But I *am* on board with this party idea. So, do you want to have it here? Maybe at Central Park? No muggers this year."

I smiled. It was our family joke from the first day in Sundog. Just a block and a half from our house was a leafy, peaceful city park called Central Park that had been established when the town was platted. Unlike the park with the same name made of vast acres of trees and paths in New York City, this one was positively petite. It was one block square, with sidewalks all around and two sidewalks that crossed in the very center like a huge concrete "X." At the fulcrum of the "X" was a circle of paving stones, about thirty feet in diameter with a waist high stone wall defining its quadrants. Inside the circle was a natural amphitheater, and sometimes a vintage band concert or a poetry reading was held there. Outside the stone walls were beds filled with a mix of perennials and annuals—bleeding hearts, peonies, tulips, daffodils, and black-eyed Susans intermixed with petunias, marigolds, snapdragons, pansies, and zinnias. Mom and I had helped on the weeding and planting day in April, and we were scheduled to weed and water one quadrant during the last two weeks of August.

"Not Central Park. I mean, it's pretty, and there are lots of picnic tables, but it doesn't seem like a place for a birthday party. You know, where you need an invitation."

"You are right. Neighbors walk by and it would be unfriendly not to invite them to sit down, but if we did it would disrupt the flow of the party."

I smiled gratefully at Mom. Sometimes she really got things right away.

"Hey!" I sat bolt upright.

"Has lightening struck?" asked Mom.

"Maybe. What about Miss Ann's pool? Do you think she would let us have the party there, on a Saturday?"

"We could ask," said Mom, cautiously.

"And, Mom?"

"Yes?"

"I know what I want for my birthday. Just in case you were stumped for fresh, enchanting-yet-educational ideas. Something without the ongoing expense of the Firefly phone."

"With a spiel like that, I have to ask. What do you have in mind?"

"A video camera." I held my breath. This was a long shot. A video camera was expensive and not really a toy.

"Hmm. Explain the sudden lust for electronics."

"Actually, it's not sudden. Not at all. I have always loved movies. You know that."

"This is true."

"Remember when I thought 'DVD' was a word without a vowel?"

"Mmmmm."

"And I have been reading this." I pulled out a copy of *Hey Kid! Make a Vid!*—a fun and fact-filled book about making videos.

"Let's see." Mom reached over and read the blurb on the back cover. "The library has lots of great books."

Clearly, she was not willing to commit herself.

"Will you at least think about it?"

"Long and hard, Alexa. Now, back to the party…"

She hadn't said no outright. At least, that was something.

Before the day was out, Miss Ann had said yes. We had the pool party all mapped out, down to the date, invitations (manila envelopes with blow-up beach balls inside), menu (hot dogs, potato chips, fresh vegetables and dip) and a super-fantastic idea for a cake. I had seen it in a magazine. It was a long sheet cake with the center removed and filled with blue gelatin to make a pool. A pool slide was made out of over-turned ice cream cones and long pieces of licorice. Little gummi bears slid down the slide and paddled in the pool, with some resting on candy Lifesavers. Mom said that she wasn't experienced with baked tableaux, but she would try. That was all I could ask.

The morning of the party dawned bright and clear. I was so excited that I wore my swimming suit and goggles to the breakfast table. Of course, I was the first one to arrive at Miss Ann's house. Dad carried the cake carefully. We had all spent the morning decorating it, and it really looked like a swimming pool if you squinted just a bit. Mom carried a wicker hamper with the rest of the food, and I carried a paper grocery bag with plates, cups, napkins, and plastic forks.

The sun was shining hard, bouncing off the blue of the swimming pool. Dad set the cake down on a table shaded by an umbrella and returned to the car. Mom and I set out the food next to the cake. Miss Ann was away for the weekend, up at her lake place, but she had given us the key so we could go inside and use the bathrooms and get water from the kitchen. She also agreed that Constanza, Eduardo's mother, who was Red Cross certified in lifesaving, could lifeguard. I unlocked the back door and went in to put an envelope with a check in it on her kitchen counter.

When I returned to the patio, Constanza and Eduardo had arrived. "*Hola*, Alexa," Constanza said. "*Feliz cumpleaños!*"

"Thanks! Hi, Zorro!" I said.

"Happy birthday," he said with a grin, handing me a package.

As I thanked him and took the gift to the table, I saw another package, a big one wrapped in shining orange paper and silver ribbon, in Dad's arms. He was lifting it down carefully. It looked heavy.

"Ed, do you mind if she opens this one first?"

"No."

"Great! We'll save the other gifts for when everyone is here, but, go ahead, Kitten. Open this one now."

As I started to pull off the zany orange paper with gold spirals and stars, my heart started to beat a little faster. I was right! It was a video camera! Dad, being Dad, had already charged the battery and made sure everything worked. There was enough time before everyone else arrived for me to skim through the quick start guide with him. I was able to film an entire parade of friends, bearing gifts. Then it was time for food, and I was starving, so I put the camera down and filled up my plate with lunch.

After lunch, we had to wait for 30 minutes before we could go in the water. Even though it is a myth that you can get cramps with a full stomach, my parents like to play it safe. Clean up only took about three minutes. Then we played a fun (for me) pencil game, seeing how many words could be made from "Happy Birthday, Alexa!" The winner was Isabelle, and she was awarded the prize of a red leather CD case, which made her smile. (The best words, in my opinion, were "Earth" and "axle.")

Then I let my friends play around with the camera a bit, telling jokes, pretending to interview famous people (but just each other really). That all took about ten minutes.

Mom said, "We're going to wait to cut the cake until after swimming. But why don't we light the candles and sing now? Then we can open presents before everyone is all wet."

"Hurray!" shouted everyone, including me. I didn't want to appear greedy or anything, but wrapped-up presents always make me curious, even if they are not for me. When they are for me, my curiosity goes sky-high, just like mercury rising in a thermometer. I think the other kids felt the same way.

"Here," said Ursula. "Open my gift first." I thanked her and, remembering my manners, opened the card first. It was a Snoopy one, perfect for my first summer in Minnesota, I thought, since Charles Schulz had been born here way back in the last century. Then I pulled off the zebra paper and hot pink ribbons to find a Swiss Army knife!

"This is so cool!" I shouted.

Ursula smiled. "We can use it in the woods."

Otto was practically dancing with excitement. "Now mine," he said, handing me his gift. It was a cloth tote bag with an elephant on it. I looked inside. Everything was green: a small soccer ball, a round doughnut-shaped piece of polished green marble on a black silk cord, like a portable Blarney stone (the card, with a picture of an Irish harp on it, said the stone was from Connemara), and a little green glass ring shaped like a shamrock.

"These are to make you think of Ireland," Otto explained, "and Irish dancing."

"I get that. They are really nice," I said as I slipped the necklace over my head. "They make me think of you, too." I held my arms down at my side and danced a little jig. Those summer dance classes were keeping my feet springy.

"Are there lots of elephants in Ireland?" asked Eduardo, rather sarcastically.

"No, silly. Alexa just likes elephants."

It was true. I am in awe of elephants. "An adult elephant has 40,000 separate muscles in its trunk," I said. "Just imagine a nose with that kind of flexibility and power!"

But no one else was in the mood to digress.

"Here." Eduardo handed me his gift: an upside-down wizard hat. It was midnight blue, covered with gold stars and crescent moons. It had a big flooooff of white tissue paper at the top, so it looked like an ice cream cone for an alchemist. I reached underneath the paper and drew out a book called "Card Tricks for Beginners" and a new slippery deck of cards with a red-eyed loon on the back of each.

"It's Minnesota's state bird," offered Eduardo.

"Yeah, and you're kind of a loon sometimes," teased Otto.

I put the wizard hat on Otto. He looked just like a garden gnome. We all laughed, including him.

"Thanks," I said to Eduardo. "You have to promise to teach me some good ones."

"Okay."

Then Isabelle, who was a patient waiter, handed me two oblong packages wrapped in floral paper awash with pinks, blues, yellows, and greens. The two packages were tied together with raffia.

I pulled off the ribbon and handed it to Mom, then ripped off the paper. I have never had the patience to unwrap a gift carefully enough to save the paper. The smaller one was a box of woodless colored pencils, just the kind I had admired Isabelle using. The larger package was a really cool book on how to make any kind of hat—Egyptian pharaoh's wig, British judge's wig, pioneer girl poke bonnet—from grocery bags and construction paper, tape, glue, and paint.

"Wow!" I hugged her impetuously. "This is the basis for my whole wardrobe department at Alexa Studios! When we make our first movie, we'll be all set."

Then it was time for swimming. We were planning to jump right in, but Mom said, "Wait! Wait! We need a group picture."

She got her camera out and took off the lens cover.

Then I had an even better idea! This was going to be historic, so I asked Dad to use my new video camera to film us. Then I walked out to the end of the diving board and sat down. Behind me came Isabelle and Otto. They sat down, too, with their legs dangling over the side. Isabelle rested her chin on my right shoulder, and Otto rested his chin on my left shoulder. Then came Ursula, who knelt behind, making devil's horns with her fingers over my head. Last came Eduardo with his arms outstretched like Frankenstein's monster, until he reached Ursula. Then he lifted his arms high above his head and clasped his hands together like a champion boxer after a match.

Mom was snapping pictures like crazy. Dad was smiling behind the video camera. The sun was warm and bright. I was so happy I thought I might burst—so happy I didn't care if I did. I was ten years old at last, and I had amazing friends, two things for which I had waited my entire life.

"Hey, everybody! Let's have a big old birthday howl!" I raised my chin and led off the pack in fine style. The gang joined in immediately. But we couldn't keep it up for long because we started laughing. Pretty soon, we had all slipped into the water and were dog-paddling around and giggling.

It was the best birthday party I had ever had. I was sorry when parents started showing up to collect my guests.

Later, when we were back at the house, I reviewed the video tape of the day. Right before we all fell off the diving board, my dad's laugh broke over the tape saying "Look! Five vowels, all howling!"

And so from then on we were called the Howling Vowels.

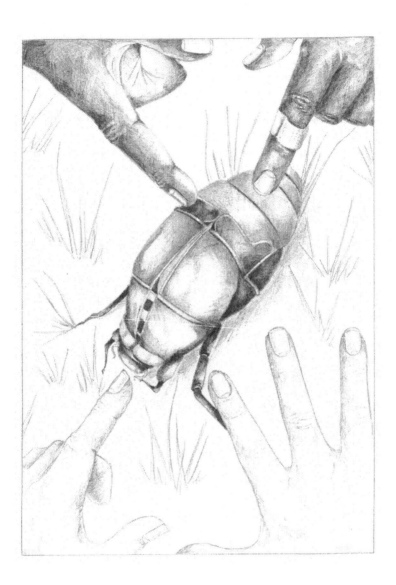

Chapter Seven
"Fair Weather Friends"

O ne hot day, in early August, I lay on the Chinese carpet in the living room, wrestling with a puzzle. I was completely engrossed in searching for the word "terrapin" in the word scramble, when I heard a soft snorting sound. As I looked up, I heard it again.

Dad was stretched out on the couch with a baseball cap drawn over his eyes and a translation of *The Odyssey* resting open on his stomach. His inhalations were silent, but his exhalations made it sound as if a friendly bison were sleeping in our living room.

I tried to ignore it, but pretty soon it was all I could think about. So I did what had to be done: I very quietly took the end of my braid and ran it up and down on the sole of Dad's foot, tickling him into wakefulness. He gave a little yelp. Then Odysseus, Penelope, the swine, suitors, and all took a short, violent luge ride that ended with a smack on the hard wood floor.

I laughed. It's fun to tease Dad.

"No fair," he protested, frowning.

"I'm sorry," I said, and partly I meant it. "But you sounded like Shrek."

"Then I think 'This is the part where *you* run away,'" he whispered with something approaching a Scottish accent. He made a grab for me. I shrieked and darted around the coffee table. I am quick but Dad has long arms, and pretty soon he was tickling me under the arm, just like I thought he would. Dad is a great tickler, because he never does it so long that it becomes mean. One way Dad and I are the same is that we both like to laugh. And when I am tickled by Dad, I am filled with laughter the way a hot air balloon is filled with helium.

"Scoop?" I said when I caught my breath.

"Oh, Kitten. I am getting on in years, you know," he said. "So are you," he added. "You're ten now."

"Scoop?"

"Well, okay, if you jump like a rocket off a launch pad and save my increasingly creaky knees."

I nodded happily. Dad put his hands under my arms, and I shouted, "One. Two. Three. Blast-off!" and Dad scooped me high into the air into a big hug, just like he had been doing my whole life. I didn't like to think that there might come a day when I would be too big to be scooped up by my dad. So I changed the subject.

"Say, Dad?"

"Yep?"

"I have an idea."

"That's a new one," he said, putting me down and tapping his forehead with his finger. "Alexa with an idea. Okay, shoot."

"Two words. Science Fair! What do you think?"

"I'm intrigued. I'm intrigued. But I am going to need more than two words before I render an opinion from on high in my stentorian tones."

Both Dad and Mom can tend toward the verbally dramatic end of the curve, if you know what I mean. They say it is in self-defense. Anyway...

"Dad, Stentor had a voice as loud as fifty men. I think you exaggerate."

"I never exaggerate. I merely embellish."

He never lets up either, unless you distract him.

"We could have an exhibit on megaphones. At the science fair. Assuming we get it off the ground."

"We? Are you perhaps referring to... *moi*?

"Well, yeah."

"How about we just go to the State Fair? You aren't a real Minnesotan until you've done that. Oh! I can see it now! Ferris wheels and bungee jumping. Corn dogs and mini doughnuts. Emus, llamas, and all the basic farmyard animals. And crop art! All those little seeds glued into astounding approximations of springing cougars, prairie sunsets, and the unmistakable face of Garrison Keillor."

I patted his arm. "That sounds great, Dad. But the State Fair isn't until the end of August. We need to do something right now."

"We do?"

"Yeah." I nestled against his side. "I'm missing our usual August. I woke up thinking about Block Island. Swimming. Looking for shells and driftwood. Making fires on the beach."

"We'll go to Block Island again sometime. Maybe next summer." He started down the hall to the kitchen. I followed at his elbow.

"I know. The move was expensive. We just can't afford the money or the time this year. I do get it, Dad. I don't mean to complain. But there is a great big hole in August, right where Block Island used to be."

"You need to remap August?" Dad took off his cap and hung it on a hook in the hall, then strode into the kitchen.

"Yep."

"So, what do your friends think about a science fair? This sounds more like a kid thing than a dad and daughter do." Dad lifted the red kettle off the counter, made sure it was full of water, and set it on the burner. Then he unleashed the gas flames. I always liked the surprise of the color blue licking at the red enameled metal, as if the kettle were already hot and the flames were as cool as water.

"Well," I looked at the end of my braid. From one angle it looked like a paint brush. From another it looked like a sawed-off piece of rope. I began lashing it back and forth like a tiger's tail. "I am not sure that the other Howling Vowels would be all that interested."

Just saying that out loud made me feel sad and all alone. Yesterday, when the idea first came to me, I was over at Otto's house shooting hoops. It was hot and sticky. Both of us had worked up a sweat. Brigid called from the deck, "Young'uns! Come up for a cool drink. I get faint simply looking at you."

Otto gave me his goofy grin and wiped off his forehead with the edge of his T-shirt. "Phew! She's right. Let's get some water."

"Okay."

We passed from the driveway onto the grass and followed the herbaceous border that curved back toward the deck. The flowerbed was Brigid's pride and joy. Even in August, when most of the neighborhood lawns were burnt brown and what flowers remained were shaggy with seed pods, Brigid's flowers gleamed.

Magenta hollyhocks nodded over the stand of rudbeckia, school-bus bright with stiff orange-yellow petals and centers like ground coffee beans. Russian sage floated infinitesimal clouds of lavender blooms on pale green foliage while, nearest to the grass, bursts of neon moss roses—fuchsia, white, orange, and zinger yellow—vied with the serenity of the white-splotched snow-on-the-mountain. I never got tired of drinking in the beauty of Brigid's flowers, set off carefully from each other by neat, dark patches of newly cultivated soil.

Suddenly, something caught my eye.

"Wow! Look at this!" I said to Otto. He came over and bent down to see what I was pointing at.

"That's just a cicada shell. Casing. I don't know what you call it."

"These are cicadas? I read all about them in New York, but I didn't know this was their year."

"It's just some insect."

"No, Otto. It is a once-in-seventeen-years-phenomenon. I didn't know we could have insects *this big* in Sundog? It looks like something that belongs in a tropical rain forest."

"Yep. Well, it's kind of unusual, I guess."

"I'll say. Have you researched it? Have these always been indigenous? Are they Asian imports? Do they cause any damage? Will they hurt your mom's flowers? Just think—the last time they were here we weren't even born."

Otto had wandered into the kitchen before me. I was following him, when I had my brilliant idea. I stopped, and stood still. I actually looked up to see whether there was a light bulb above my head. "Otto! I've got it!"

He backed out of the kitchen, like those old videos of Michael Jackson moon walking.

"What?"

"It's perfect. We'll have a science fair! It will be so cool. We can do a display about insects. And maybe Eduardo would do some of the physics behind his magic tricks. Maybe your mom would help us explain about how flowers are made, you know, how that the plant knows when it is time to make the bud." I had a lot more to say, but Otto cut me off.

"Whoa, Alexa. You make my head hurt."

He went in the kitchen again—not moon walking. I followed and had a drink of water, too. But I am not the type to take "No" for an answer, and so I kept trying to persuade him. Nothing worked, though.

When I pressed him to say why he wasn't interested, he said, "Jeez, Alexa! It's only August. School doesn't start for another month. Why don't you let me enjoy what's left of my summer, okay?"

The more I tried to explain how fun it would be to learn something new, the more Otto didn't want to hear it. Finally, he said that he had to practice the piano. But he doesn't even take lessons, so I knew that he was trying to find a nice way to ask me to go home.

So I left. Boy, did I feel lower than dirt. Just when I thought I had found a place where I could be my whole self—here in Sundog among so many great friends—I didn't fit after all. Why couldn't Otto see how cool a science fair would be?

The next morning, when I got up, I couldn't get the science fair idea out of my head. I thought about calling up Isabelle, to see what she thought, but she was gone for a couple of days to her grandparents out near Pipestone. Then I thought about calling Ursula or Eduardo, but something stopped me. It was remembering Otto, not looking at me, shaking his head. So when Otto called to ask me to bike over to the swimming pool, I said no and settled down with some brain teasers instead. Still, the more I tried to forget it, the more I was puzzled. A science fair *was* a good idea. How come nobody but me could see that?

The red kettle whistled, then shrieked. Dad turned off the flame, flipped back the spout cover, and poured boiling water into his mug. "Have you asked the gang?" he inquired.

"I've only talked with Otto. He thinks it's too much like school."

"Oh. I see." Dad dunked his tea bag rhythmically, up and down, up and down by its skinny string. I found it hypnotic.

Finally Dad lifted the tea bag clear of the mug and dropped it in a small dish near the stove. Carrying his steaming brew, he headed back to the living room. "Let's strategize," he said over his shoulder.

I followed. "You think I should ask the other kids, don't you?"

Dad nodded as he sipped. Then he said, "I don't think you'll enjoy it if you go it alone. Or even just with my help. This is a group activity for kids if I ever heard of one.

"So," he continued, "I think you need to present this idea to your friends. And I think you'll be more successful if you include plenty of room for their ideas."

"I *always* listen to other people's ideas," I protested, then amended, truthfully, "The good ones, anyway."

Dad lifted one eyebrow in that quizzical way he has and looked at me levelly.

I sighed. "Maybe you have a point."

"In the spirit of science, Kitten," he said, "see what happens. Everyone has good ideas, but some people's aren't quite so near the surface as yours. They need a bit of encouragement—a bit of space—to share them."

He settled more deeply into his chair. "But one thing I do know: most people have more enthusiasm for developing their own ideas than for fetching and carrying in the service of someone else's grand plan."

I nodded. "Thanks, Dad."

"Anytime."

On my way to the phone, I picked up the Find-A-Word puzzle I'd been working on and crumpled it into a ball. My mission was "Find-A-Friend" now. Dad had told me what I needed to work on. The hardest thing of all: listening.

Do I have to say it? In fairness, yes: Dad was right. I guess I do come on a little strong sometimes. First, I went to Otto's to see if he wanted to play some more basketball, and he was glad to. I think he had been missing me. It was a little bit less muggy. After our game, we sat on his back steps with a pitcher of ice water and some Rice Krispie treats. What happened was, I didn't even have to say anything, because Otto brought up the science fair himself.

"Remember that thing you wanted to do?"

"That science fair idea?"

"Yeah."

"I remember."

"I've been thinking about it."

"Oh?"

"Yeah." Otto took a big gulp of his water and then a big bite of his Rice Krispie treat. It was maddening to me to wait while he chewed and swallowed and decided what to say, but I could see that Dad was right. I tried to channel my impatience through my fingers by twirling a clover stem, first this way, then that.

"Could be kinda cool."

"What should we do?" I could feel my skin literally itching, as if I would jump out of it from the sheer need to share my own ideas. It felt as though I were way down at the bottom of the sea. My ears were filled with the rushing sound of my own heartbeats. Those were my ideas, banging on the inside of my head. But way far away, it seemed, I could hear Otto's voice, like it was at the end of a long tunnel.

"Mom said we could have that roll of tickets in the basement. She's not going to use them. And she would make Rice Krispie treats for us to sell."

What was this? I listened a little harder. Otto's voice got clearer to me.

"And my dad said he would put up the tent if we wanted."

Otto had some great ideas. Only thing was, there was nothing about science. Did he just want a big circus thing?

"And I don't know so much about science, Alexa, but you and the others could take charge of that part."

Oh. Otto was showing himself to be a true friend. But I thought that he was selling himself short.

"I think you are great at science."

"Oh, come on."

"No, really. Come here. Bring that basketball. Let's do a little experiment. I'll prove it to you."

He followed me over to the driveway, and we stood behind the free-throw line that he had chalked across the asphalt.

"Okay. Now make a basket."

Otto squinted at the hoop and gave the big orange ball two thoughtful bounces. Then he took it in his hands and rocked back on his heels. He drew in a deep breath and as he released it, the ball soared beyond his fingertips, creating a perfect parabola before it passed through the metal hoop with the smallest swishing sound.

"See!" I said triumphantly.

"That's not science. That's just sports."

"Otto, science is everywhere. You just demonstrated the effects of gravity on an object, the complicated mechanics of the human muscular-skeletal system, the interconnectedness of hand-eye coordination, and Newton's three Laws of Motion."

"I did all that?"

"Of course you did. Science isn't a school subject, Otto. It's about trying things out and seeing what works and wondering why things are the way they are. That is what kids do all the time."

"Hmmm. What is that Newton thing?"

"The Laws of Motion?"

"Yeah."

"Well, the first one says that an object at rest tends to stay at rest, and an object in motion tends to remain in motion. I think that is it. It was so cool to see the law translated through you. The basketball was at rest in your hands, until *you* put it into motion."

Otto broke out in a big smile, but shook his head. "I don't know. I still think it's just sports, but I'm willing to play along."

"Toss me that ball!"

He did, and I dribbled it all the way to the street and back up the driveway, stopping at the free-throw line.

"Bombs, away!" I called, letting it fly. The ball bounced off the backboard, hit the front of the rim, wavered a minute, and went in.

"Yes!" I shouted, clutching my fist in to my side, then giving Otto a high five. "What I lack in elegance, I make up for in sheer drive."

Over the next few days, things lined up. Eddie and Ursula were bored with summer, too, so they jumped on the idea. Isabelle returned from nearly a week at her grandparents' lake place, and she said she would do anything to avoid being in close quarters with her twin brothers for a while.

We met at my place for a "Science Summit" to decide what to do.

Two hours later, we were knee-deep in ideas. The next Saturday, using signs, phone calls, and flyers, we had alerted the whole neighborhood to the Science Fair.

My whole front porch was turned into a museum, and we had experiments in Otto's family's tent in the back garden. Some neighbors down the block found out what we were doing and donated two *What Is It? Exhibits*: "Guess the Mysterious Kitchen Device from Days of Yore" and "How Would You Like That in Your Mouth? Obsolete Dental Instruments."

We didn't forget the refreshments. We served brownies baked in a solar oven and sips of mostly clear water that we purified from muddy water through a homebuilt sediment filtration system. They made a good combination. We also had dried apple slices to show how Isabelle's mom's food dryer worked.

Eduardo did some razzle-dazzle Guess-What-Will-Happen? physics experiments using a dust-buster, strings of crepe paper, and little rubber balls.

Ursula made a poster board display of Guinness World Records Feats of Strength. She also had her collection of local snake skins and petrified raccoon scat on display.

Isabelle demonstrated how to cut complicated lace work from paper. When her finger got tired from the scissors, she converted her booth to a challenge zone. With two Rubik's cubes and a timer, she challenged visitors to beat her time after they altered the patterns on both cubes. Secretly I dubbed her "the Blur" because she could do it so fast.

Otto sold tickets, and he kept everybody cracking up with science-related jokes that he had looked up on the Internet, like these:

What's the most important thing to learn in chemistry?
 Never lick the spoon!
What do you do when you find a dead chemist?
 Barium!
What does a sick duck say?
 Quark!
Did you know there are 10 kinds of mathematicians in the world?
 Those who understand binary and those who don't!

And me? I had made two displays. One was called "Cicada Circus." It showed the seventeen year cycle of the cicada. The centerpiece of that was the husk I had found at Otto's house. And Mom let me power her laptop to demonstrate the Wonder of Fractals for my second display. I played a great DVD that showed how fractal forms appear in ferns and coastlines and also in the kitchen! It even had an interview with Professor Benoit Mandelbrot who was the innovator of fractal mathematics. Boy, would I like to have a new discovery named after me.

Because my displays did not require any monitoring, I was free to wander around. Of course, I had my new video camera with me. It was great to see how much fun people were having. Word had gotten out, and before the day was out we had used 103 tickets (but that total included the ones that Otto handed out to the cats and dogs—he just tucked one into each pet collar). I kept having fresh ideas, like making it into a year round museum with T-shirts and posters. But I realized that that was dreaming too big for the time being. What really struck me was how creative all my friends were. Dad knew what he was talking about when he said I couldn't and shouldn't do it alone.

When the sun dipped below the trees, all the Howling Vowels gathered on our front porch. We were tired, but it had been a glorious day. I passed the video camera around, to get the view of each person. We also passed around some cream sodas and the last pan of solar brownies. Boy, when the ingredients are good, it doesn't matter much about texture, does it? They tasted great.

"Too bad the twins couldn't come. *Not!*" giggled Isabelle.

"I have really got to send away for some new tricks," mused Eduardo.

"Awesome brownies," said Ursula with a satisfied sigh as she licked her fingers.

I held my breath. What would Otto say?

"Science doesn't stink after all," said Otto.

For once, I didn't say anything.

Chapter Eight
"Spooky and Spectacular"

People in Sundog pay more attention to the seasons than do people in Manhattan. Back east, people who want to look at leaves drive to New Hampshire or Vermont. I can't believe that those New England trees are any prettier than the ones in Minnesota, though. Sundog streets are lined with pin oaks, maples, ginkgos, and lindens. The lindens go a buttery yellow, while the fan-shaped ginkgos are a hard, stiff, bright gold. The pin oaks are a lovely soft, rusty red—almost terra-cotta—while the maples (my favorites) are all kinds of shades, from yellow and orange to deep red. Some leaves even have a mix of those colors plus streaks of green, like paints all pooled together. Add to that the dark evergreens, blue spruces, white birch trunks, green grass, screaming red sumac and brilliant blue sky—well, after the concrete of Manhattan, it is quite a show.

It is like a concert, too. To think I was ten years old before I got to wade through gutters full of rustling dry leaves and jump—*Banzai!*—in a big pile of raked leaves. Well, if you've ever done this, you know what I am talking about. If you haven't, then you just can't know until you try it.

But to tell you the truth, I was even more excited about trick-or-treating. There I was, into the double digits, practically a teenager, and I had never gone trick-or-treating. Sure, I had had costumes. Mom is an artist, after all. The year I first realized how cool it would be to learn to swim—I was about six—I went as the Little Mermaid. Not a Disney version, though. I wore a turquoise body suit and we put greenish-blue theater paints on my face, hands, and hair so I could go to a party as the copper Little Mermaid in the harbor at Copenhagen. When I was six and interested in princesses, we thought my red hair made me look like Elizabeth I during her imprisonment at Hatfield House. Mom sewed rows and rows of glass pearls across the bodice of a taffeta and velvet dress modeled on a photo of a portrait we found. Another year, I went as a skeleton, in a black suit with all the bones not only painted on but labeled in their Latin names. I still have that one. And the year before we moved here, when I was deep into Lewis Carroll, Mom bought ten decks of cards and a pink plastic flamingo so that I could go as the Queen of Hearts—now, that is one scary queen, if you ask me.

But all these costumes just went to tame parties at neighbor's apartments or at Miss Prescott's School or at a club meeting. The closest I came to traditional trick-or-treating was wearing my costume to the corner market and having the checkout lady put a piece of penny candy in my hand. I wanted to come up with something really special for my first real trick-or-treating. The rest of the Vowels had great ideas, and I didn't want to let them down. I talked it over with Mom.

"Mom, I need some help," I said as she was putting a thin layer of gouache over a pre-stretched canvas.

"Mmmm?" She really wasn't paying attention.

"Mom, listen, okay? Please. *Back away from the brush.*"

She raised her eyebrows at me. It could have gone either way, but then she put the brush down and smiled. "Sorry. I *have* been a bit distracted lately. It is so exciting to have a show again, even a small Sundog show." Mom was preparing some new paintings to hang in March at the Arts Guild gallery. As far as I was concerned, March was a lifetime away.

"Thanks, Mom. It's about Halloween. All the kids have great costume ideas, but I don't know what to go as."

"Well, which ideas are already taken?"

"Isabelle is going as a Flower Fairy. She is so little, she really looks like a fairy, and she has been drying flowers all summer. Ursula's aunt sent her a complete Wonder Woman costume. She is going to get a black wig and everything. She is even practicing with the golden lasso."

"No invisible plane, though, right?"

I smiled with just one corner of my mouth at the feeble joke. "And the boys are typecast. Eduardo will go as, what else? A magician. Not all Harry Potterish. More like Houdini. His grandfather gave him a real silk cape and a top hat. And Otto is tall enough this year to wear Ed's Zorro costume from last year. I've seen it. It's great. It is from Spain, and the hat even has the little bobbles around the brim."

"So, you want something amazing, but aren't sure what?"

"That's about the size of it."

"Well, I always think better on a full stomach. Let's make some lunch and then we'll see."

I started setting the table—moving the geometry books and the half-finished collage I'd been working on over to the window seat. I used the state plates, old travel souvenirs that my great-grandparents had collected in the 1930s. I gave Mom the magenta Devils Tower plate, and I gave myself the hand-painted one of Niagara Falls rushing over the border from Canada into New York. Somewhere I had read that this was the only U.S. landmark to be moving north—about one foot every year as the rock eroded. It was fun to think of Grandma Marie and Grandpa Leslie Roy motoring around in an early Ford, collecting Navajo silver and rugs in the west, quilts in the south, antique pewter and rag carpets in New England, and commemorative plates from every state.

"So," said Mom, as she ladled the gluten-free noodles and steaming vegetable spaghetti over the roar and mist of the falls, "is there an underlying theme?"

"What do you mean?"

"Well, it sounds like all of you are going to be quite powerful, even the Flower Fairy, which could also be classified as cute, I guess, but flowers are phenomenonally strong."

"Flowers did change the face of the planet. They do regulate bees and animals to their own purposes, it's true."

"Yes. So you probably want to think of something powerful. That's the common thread."

"Right." I munched a bit of tender eggplant. "What is the most powerful deity? Odin? No..." I sprinkled a little parmesan on my noodles. Then I sat bolt upright. "Urd!" I shouted.

Mom dropped her fork and laughed. "Is that some kind of Norse 'Eureka?'"

"No, Mom, *Urd*! The Norns, remember? The Fays of Destiny? They spun the fate of everyone, even the gods, even Odin. Urd was the eldest of the Nornir. What could be stronger than Fate, after all?"

"Free will?"

"No, Mom. Not in Norse mythology, anyway. I've got to see Mrs. Davenport right away."

Mom was smiling as she reached over and patted my arm. "After lunch is soon enough, A."

"Oh." I saw I was standing up. "Okay. Maybe I'll call first."

"That's a good idea."

By Halloween, after several secret conferences with Mrs. Davenport and one with Mom, I was ready. Otto and the rest of the Howling Vowels were planning to call for me at 6:30 p.m. Somehow, for two whole weeks, I had managed not to talk about my costume with the gang. I wanted it to be a surprise. Instead, we had talked about where the best candy could be found. We had our route all planned. And at 6:25 p.m., I was ready for my first trick-or-treating spook night.

My face and neck and hands were painted a silvery grey-green. I had blue eyeliner around my eyes and my lips had a thick coat of zinc-based sunscreen, so they were white, and I even painted my tongue green with food coloring. I had a wig of shiny, silvery-white hair that hung down to my waist, covering all my natural red.

Mom had dyed some old sheets black, then painted them here and there with some other colors—purple, green, blue, silver. Because Urd lived at the base of Yggdrasil, the world tree, I wore a garland of green leaves on my head, and I had a bag of brown bark cloth to put candy in. Looped over my shoulders, were several strands of thick, white twine, to signify the fates of men. I walked down the stairs slowly, trying to appear as if I were floating.

Dad's eyes bugged out when he saw me, but he pretended like it was no big deal. "So, are you going as a beauty queen this year, Kitten?"

Mom gave Dad a little thump on his chest with the heel of her hand. "Honestly, Paul." To me she said, "Alexa, you've outdone yourself."

Just then the doorbell rang.

Mom went over to the door and opened it.

"Trick or Treat!" shouted four voices all together.

"Come in, come in," said Mom as she ushered my friends into the living room. "Now stay right here until I get my camera," she called over her shoulder as she headed into the den.

I held my breath to keep quiet. Then they saw me. Isabelle just stared. Ursula gave a grunt. Otto dropped his orange plastic pumpkin. Eduardo gave a low whistle.

That's how I knew that my costume had succeeded. I let out my breath.

"What are you?" asked Isabelle. "A ghoul?" Her flower petals fluttered.

"She's a witch, a *bruja*," said Eduardo with a rustle of his cape.

"Naw, a zombie," said Otto, "a *Creature from the Crypt*." The bobbles on Eduardo's Zorro hat trembled just a little.

"Wrong, wrong, and wrong!" I sang out delightedly. "What about you, Ursula? Do you want to guess?"

"Knowing you, it is something from a myth, but I don't know what." Ursula stood with her feet firmly planted and her hands on her hips. Golden bands gleamed on her wrists. She looked just like Wonder Woman. "A gorgon?" she guessed.

"Close! It is from mythology, but Norse mythology. Give up? I'm *Urd*!" I explained all about the Norns. I could tell they thought it was a cool idea.

"Well, it doesn't matter if people know Urd, because you are really creepy, Alexa," said Eduardo. "I bet it will be even weirder looking under the street lights. I know! We'll ring the bells and then when people are smiling and handing out the candy, we can step aside and you can give them a good scare."

"Great idea!" said Ursula, who enjoyed the spooky side of Halloween more than any of us.

Mom returned with her camera and herded us all into a photographable cluster. After she was done, we headed out.

The almost full moon hung in the east like a big wheel of golden Gouda cheese. It was brisk out, but we ran, shrieking, so quickly from house to house that we didn't even feel the cold. One lady told us that our cheeks were as red as apples, though I don't think she meant me because my makeup was opaque. Since the five of us were together, our parents all permitted us to go without a chaperone, and it was an unusual feeling to be out after dark with just kids. It seemed fairly spooky, even though I knew Sundog was a safe place.

At all the houses we visited, everyone thought my costume was scary, especially a couple of little kids whom I scared inadvertently. I forgot about the makeup I had on, so when I saw a little boy and his sister having trouble with an untied shoe lace, I went over to help.

"Hi, can I..." I didn't even get to finish my sentence. They both screamed and ran up the sidewalk about twenty feet where their father was waiting. He had a baby in a carrier on his back, and suddenly his arms where filled with those two.

"Cripes," I said to the Vowels. "Let's go the other way."

"Cool," said Ursula.

"They'll probably have nightmares for weeks," added Eduardo.

We went methodically over a nine-block grid, skipping only the park and the houses that had dark porch lights. By my count, we rang nearly a hundred doorbells. The spookiest thing was to go up to a house in disguise. The only people besides the Davenports who guessed it was me behind the makeup deduced it because they recognized Isabelle or Ursula or one of the boys. I guess it is true that people know you from the company you keep.

When our sacks were heavy with candy and our toes and fingers started to be nipped by the cold, we all returned to my house for hot cider. I was struck by how spooky, yet inviting, our house looked with the glow of three orangey pumpkins on the steps, the windows curtained but golden, a plump moon overhead, all these illuminating the inky blackness that felt as palpable as a sleek black cat stroking us from all sides. I wondered whether my video camera could capture that. Would the light levels register anything? I decided to try. As soon as we all got indoors, I headed for the back room shelf where my camera had its home.

"It's Stephen King!" mocked Dad when he saw what I was doing.

"You mean Alfred Hitchcock," corrected Vernon, Otto's dad, adding, "Watch out for any ferocious pigeons!" as I left the lighted safety of the indoors, went out into the black night, and started dreaming behind the lens of my camera.

Chapter Nine
"Deeper"

The next day it was November already. It got off to a quiet start. We cleaned up a few smashed pumpkins, and then I did some work on the Norwegian grammar that Mrs. Davenport was tutoring me in. It was also another holiday, one that was brand new to me. Mom said I could be excused from everything that morning including school and regular chores. Sure, I had read about *El Día de los Muertos* before. Señora Raoul from New York City had told me about it, but it had never really caught my attention before. And I was a little confused about the dates—was it November 1st or November 2nd? It turns out there are two holidays: *El día de los Angelitos* (The day of the little angels) that falls with All Saints Day on November 1st, followed by All Souls Day or the Day of the Dead on November 2nd. Finally! I understood why Halloween is called All Hallow's Eve, because it is the night before All Saints Day.

This year, being friends with Eduardo, I was intrigued. Eddie's parents invited me to come with them to the little cemetery next to the Church of Saint

Angelina, just across the river and up the hill from my neighborhood.

It was a chilly, bright day. When the Suarez family pulled into the driveway in their shiny blue Prius, I was already waiting for them on the porch. I had a tote bag with my camera, an extra battery pack, a fresh loaf of bread (courtesy of Dad), and the last of the marigolds from our garden (courtesy of Mom).

"*Hola*," said Señor Suarez. "Could you sleep at all after that feast of candy and all those scary creatures out last night?"

"I never have problems sleeping," I said, truthfully. I don't. I hate to think about going to bed, but as soon as my eyes are closed the dreams start rolling. "Do you, Zorro?" I asked, as I climbed in beside him and buckled my seatbelt.

"Nah," said Eduardo. He seemed quieter than usual, though.

"We have packed a fine lunch," said Señora Suarez, "and it looks like we will have a beautifully clear day. Not too cold."

"Yes," said Señor Suarez, "and it takes hardly any time to travel to the graves. Not like in Barcelona, eh, Constanza?"

"That is so," sighed Señora Suarez. She looked out the window and said, softly, "Here the graves are much closer to us."

About a minute later we were there. I took my tote bag. Señor Suarez opened the trunk of the car and lifted out an enormous picnic basket. Eddie carried some folding chairs and a red and green blanket. Señora Suarez, her arms full of green leaves and marigolds of many colors—bright yellow; orange; dark, bricky red— led the way as we stepped on the crazy quilt of limestone paving stones and through the gate.

The cemetery was a lovely place any day. It was about a hundred years old. Lots of trees, from bur oaks with rattly dry leaves to dark green arbor vitae pointed to the sky. On the thick grass, still green, were rows of headstones and a few small marble structures that I learned later were called mausoleums.

Lots of other families were already there, setting up chairs, unfurling blankets, arranging flowers and food against the grey stones. Children were running around with balloons and noise makers; some were wearing masks to make them look like skeletons. Grownups were unscrewing the tops of stainless steel coffee flasks. The rich smell of coffee floated on the chill air.

We wound our way around the people and behind the headstones, weaving through the living and the dead, until we came to the newest part of the graveyard. Here the trees cast less shade, the grass was more thick and green, and the carvings easier to decipher. When Señora Suarez sat gracefully down beside a grave, we all stopped. When I read the inscription, surrounded by deeply carved daisies, I dropped my marigolds.

THE HOWLING VOWELS

Marguerita Juanita Suarez
Hija adorada
de Constanza y Victor Suarez
June 6, 2007 to March 3, 2009
Requiescat in pace

I never knew that Eduardo had a little sister. He never said anything. No one did. But it must be. Señora Suarez bent over the grave like a lily. I think her eyes were closed and she was saying a prayer.

I bent over to pick up the marigolds I had dropped, but Eddie pulled on my sleeve.

"Come on," he whispered. I followed him over to the fence.

"You had a sister?"

"Yeah."

"I'm sorry."

"Yeah."

We stood there a moment, side by side, looking to the east, over the fence, down the hill, all the way to the river. Today the Bucklehorn reflected the high white cirrus clouds on its silver surface. Then, Eddie spoke without turning.

"She had leukemia. She was really sick for a while. She lost all her hair."

"I'm sorry," I said again. I really didn't know what else to say.

"It's okay."

But it wasn't okay. It wasn't okay for babies to die before they even got a chance to grow up. And I didn't know what to say or do. I wanted to make Eddie feel better, but *I* felt like I had left the house to go to a party and wound up at a funeral instead. I mean, I knew that I was going to a cemetery, but I just didn't think about what it meant, you know?

"Mom comes here a lot. I don't. I like to think about my sister before she got sick. When she laughed and smiled. Not, you know..." He made a helpless fluttering gesture toward the earth.

I did know. Even though it was natural, I didn't like to think about what happened under the ground. I noticed that one stemless marigold had caught in my sleeve. I twirled it between my thumb and fingers, just for something to do.

"Alexa?"

"Yes?"

"I am sorry, too."

"You are? Why?"

"Well," Eduardo hesitated, then said, "I was supposed to tell you before. They think I did tell you about Marguerita when I asked you to come. But I didn't, 'cause I thought you might not want to."

"Oh. That's okay." I really did understand. He didn't need to say anything else.

"Hey," he said, "are you hungry?"

"Sure," I said. To my surprise, it was true. A minute before my stomach had felt knotted and bunched. Now I was famished.

"C'mon!" Eduardo punched me lightly on the shoulder and jogged off. I followed. He led me back to his parents.

Señora Suarez was arranging all the flowers. She smiled over her shoulder at us. "Alexa, thank you for these beautiful marigolds. They are the traditional flower."

"They are holy flowers in India, too."

"Are they? I didn't know." She pulled some daisies from the picnic basket. "These I had to get from the florist. They were the namesake for our daughter. But I like that most of the flowers here are from our gardens."

I wondered if I should say something, but before I could decide, she continued, "Here!" Then she handed me a big pastry box. "Open it."

I did. Inside were tiny skulls made of sugar. Each one was different, with colored sugar hats and flowers, even some with earrings.

"Wow!" I said.

"I made some of these," Eduardo said shyly. "This one is for you." He pointed to a skull with red braids and a crown of candy flowers.

"Thanks," I told him.

"Please, my hands are not so clean," said Eduardo's mother. "Would you put them on this plate?

Except for the one with the daisies. That goes here for Marguerita."

For several minutes we worked together to spread out the picnic blanket and set out the food. Eddie had accompanied his father back to the car. Just as we had everything set up, they returned with a baby doll dressed as an angel, even down to the halo and little wings.

"Here, Mama," said Eddie. He handed the doll to his mother. She solemnly lifted it into place in the center of the circle of marigolds, then leaned the long-stemmed daisies against the doll's arms and placed the candied skull at her feet, a little to the left. I had never seen anything like it, and I found it weird, beautiful, and sad. It made me wonder. If I died, what would my parents do? I had never thought about that before.

"Here, Alexa, please have a seat." Señor Suarez gestured to the picnic blanket. "I think we older ones will stay with chairs," he said.

Eddie reached over to the platter of candy skulls, picked one up, and munched it down. "Yum," he said, wiping the sugar from his lips with the back of his hand. So I did the same. Pretty soon, we were eating all kind of things in no particular order—all new things to me. Somewhere in the distance, someone began to play a guitar. I began to relax and enjoy myself.

"Alexa," Eddie said, as the day tilted into the afternoon.

"Yes?"

"Just... I'm glad you're here."

I smiled at him. "Me, too."

Later, when I sensed things were about to wind down, I walked back over to the fence to collect my thoughts. The sun had moved behind my head. The Bucklehorn was golden and blue now. The clouds had disappeared. I took out my video camera and filmed the water for a while as it lazily flowed through town, reflecting the bridge and the building, buoying up ducks and yellow birch leaves.

Then, even though I felt shy, I began to slowly turn, until I had captured 360 degrees of that place and time. I tried to get it all: the white hair of the grandfathers and grandmothers; Eddie's parents sitting in their lawn chairs holding hands; the cascade of flowers, the flickering of candles in their glass chimneys; the candied skulls and angels and the joyful shrieks of the children. I even tried to pick up the ants that marched over the edges of the blankets and plates searching for sweet crumbs.

I could understand it all later. If I were lucky, that is. Right now, my job was to keep my eyes wide open.

Chapter Ten
"Thanksgiving Cornucopia"

U ntil that first year in Sundog, I thought of Thanksgiving less as a holiday and more of a long weekend, on the same level with Memorial Day and Labor Day. With Mom being an orphan and Dad's family being so far away in Minnesota, it was just the three of us. None of us like turkey. Our traditions just weren't... *traditional*. On Thanksgiving Day, we'd have city food—onion bagels, broccoli fried rice, cannoli— and loaf around until afternoon. Usually we looked through the paper, then did a brand new 1,000 piece jigsaw puzzle.

I was never interested in standing with thousands of people in the cold to see the Macy's Day Parade down in Herald Square. Sometimes we watched it on television. Then, about four o'clock, we'd go out for Chinese food and catch a movie. On Friday, which lots of people regard as a shopping day, Mom would start organizing us for Christmas. We'd make out our Christmas lists, pull the boxes of decorations out of storage, and start to address the envelopes for the cards we'd made earlier in the summer. (When your Mom is both an artist and very organized, cards get her top billing on the yuletide round-up. Dad says he is most interested in the Christmas food. Me, I like the presents best.)

In Sundog, though, people are more traditional. They actually talk about cranberries and groaning boards. And, of course, ironing boards. White linen table cloths are unfolded, aired, and smoothed. Silver and crystal are polished. Doors are decorated with Indian corn and wreaths constructed of sage leaves and tiny squash.

Aware of all this, I was wondering how my family would spend Thanksgiving. It was less than two weeks away.

"Mom?"

Mom was wearing the little frown she wore when she tried to pay bills without putting on her glasses. The woman can be a little bit vain, and it is doubly surprising to me because she actually looks good in her glasses, which are very slender with green enamel. Those glasses make me wish I had astigmatism. Maybe when I hit middle age and require reading glasses I can wear Mom's, because they will certainly still be in mint condition.

"Can we have turkey for Thanksgiving this year?"

"You hate turkey."

"But it's traditional."

"But you won't eat it. You say the smell of it makes you puke."

"I know, but it is Thanksgiving."

"*Right.* I'll be polishing that gravy boat tonight, then."

Honestly. Mom switches back and forth. Sometimes she is the irresistible force. Sometimes she is the immoveable object. Now she had a set to her jaw as though she'd been carved onto the side of Mount Rushmore: four dead presidents and Mom, none of them budging an inch.

"Well, what are we having?"

"I haven't started to think about it yet."

"Well, when will you *start?*"

Mom sighed in exasperation. I knew that she was preparing for a show of her work at the Sundog Art Center. Her new friend, Myrna, and she were collaborating. I felt bad about bothering her, but that wouldn't be until March. This was important, too. Finally, Mom put down her pen and rubbed her temples. "Okay, A., my darling. Let's talk menus. Thanksgiving is a time of celebration?"

"Check."

"Whatever you think of the myth of Squanto and kindly Pilgrims, there is a real core of heartfelt thanks for a good harvest."

"Check. And don't forget the gratitude for thriving in a new land."

"The fog begins to lift, Number One Daughter. You rather like it here in quiet Sundog. Despite the occasional whining about the lack of good delis, great shopping, and world-class museums?"

"Triple check. Those urban advantages are great, Mom. I do miss the city sometimes. But I just love Sundog, and I was so afraid that I wouldn't, you know? I didn't want to say it to you, or especially to Dad, since he was so excited..."

Mom gave me one of her deep looks. "I do know. And Dad knows, too. To tell you the truth, he was a bit worried about both of his green-eyed ladies."

Once I had her attention, Mom accelerated fast into project mode. Before we knew it, there were cookbooks all over the dining room table. In just a minute more, it seemed, we had a draft menu in front of us, a check list of tasks, and a tentative timeline.

"Phew!" Mom blew a little puff of air that lifted her bangs. Her face was pink and her eyes sparkled. She'd never admit it, probably, but she likes to tackle a challenge, especially one with an aesthetic component. "Now, what about decorations? And a guest list?" Mom asked.

"Decorations? Sure. We could put something on the table and hang something on the door. But I wasn't thinking about any guests. Who would we even invite?" I questioned.

"If we are going this deep into the Thanksgiving experience, we ought to invite others in. That is part of the tradition, sharing the feast with those outside the family walls. But you are right. Most people already have their own plans. Let me think about this."

Hmmm. This had taken an unforeseen turn. I wasn't sure that I wanted to have other people be part of it. I don't know why, but it just wasn't what I pictured.

The next day, when I came down for breakfast, Mom hung up the phone and turned to me excitedly.

"We have guests!"

I got an immediate knot in my stomach. "Yeah?" I said. "Who?"

"Well, first I called Brigid, but they have plans. So do the Suarez family and Myrna; she will be going to her daughter's house this year. But the Davenports don't have plans, and they will be most pleased to join us. Also, Ursula and her dad will come. That poor man sounded incredibly relieved to have somewhere to go without a long drive. I am calling Isabelle and her mom and dad next. The last time I talked to Frances, she was working so many shifts in the E.R. that the thought of the holidays was getting her down."

"Okay. You, me, and Daddy are three. Add Ursula and her dad, plus the Davenports, that's seven. Frances, Kevin, Isabelle, and the twins. That makes twelve. We'll have a full house. Thank heaven for Aunt Margie's dining room things. Daddy was right to insist we store them all those years. You know, Alexa, I am beginning to enjoy the idea."

"It's nice of you to go to all this trouble, Mom," I started to say.

"No one can plan a party like your mother, A. Am I right?"

"Yeah," I confirmed in a weak voice.

"When I am right, I am right. In fact, let's all break into a rousing chorus of my favorite song: *Mom Was Right!*" said Mom.

I slumped my head onto the table and groaned. She snapped her fingers and danced around singing a song she made up years ago. I have to hand it to the woman, she can really belt it out when she wants to.

"Well, Ethel Merman I'm not," said Mom, leaning up against the counter and fanning herself with the take-out menu from the Mandarin Gardens. "Phew!" she said again.

"Sheesh!" I said. I was still in a bit of a bad temper.

"Oh, come on, A. You'll like having a big crowd. These are all people you know and like. I don't understand what the big deal is."

I didn't really know, either. I knew for sure that there was no way to change things, so the only possible course was to make the best of it. What else can you do when you have inadvertently stepped on the trip wire that releases your mother's manic side? But I surprised myself by suddenly falling into a fit of homesickness for

New York, when holidays meant just the three of us all cozy on the couch, with the traffic far below and all the lights of the whole city pooling in, creating a rainbow of color on the surface of the Hudson River. The way it used to be suddenly shimmered in my memory like the evanescent bridge to Aasgaard, home of the Norse gods, and it was just as impossible to cross.

A few days later, after completing my pre-algebra problems for the week, I went down to the kitchen for a drink of water. Mom's desk was tucked into one corner of the spacious kitchen. Her computer was on and the printer was humming. Mom was humming, too.

"Hello, darling," she said with a smile. "Just look what I have found on the web." She scrolled down to a beautifully arranged photograph of a turkey resting on a shiny silver platter. "We have a lot of decisions to make regarding the stuffing."

"We do?"

"Yes! Just listen. There's a basic sage and bread crumbs one. Here's one that sounds good, with red onions, gorgonzola, and walnuts. Or how about this one with tarragon, truffles, and rye toast? Who knew?"

"So," I leaned on the counter, trying to inject a casual tone into my voice. "Have you heard back from anyone we invited?"

"Yes. Good news. Everyone said yes."

I groaned inwardly.

"Stop sagging, Alexa. You set the wheels in motion. And you will have Ursula and Isabelle to giggle with."

That was true.

"We'll make sure that those cute twin boys are occupied, so they don't bother you girls," she added, thoughtfully. "You know, I think it will be the first time you three girls have been together without any boys."

Hmmm. That could be really fun.

"But, Mom?"

"Yes."

"What about our old traditions?"

"You mean sitting around on the couch?"

"Well, yeah."

"How about if we do that on Friday? I think Dad is even planning to buy a new puzzle."

That cheered me up.

The next few days were very busy. Mom and I cleaned the house from "stem to stern" as she put it. Must have been her old Yankee roots coming out, because to my knowledge she'd never set foot on a sailing vessel. But we were definitely embarked upon an adventure. It was fun to pore over recipes and make a special trip to Trader Joe's in the Cities to buy just the right bitter almond cookies for the chocolate refrigerator cake. We shined silver and polished woodwork with lemon oil. We borrowed a fantastically long white linen table cloth from Mrs. Davenport and draped it over

Aunt Margie's mahogany table, transforming it into a blank canvas.

On Wednesday evening, we ate supper at the kitchen table. Not that that was so unusual. Despite having a studio in the attic, Mom often had an art project spread out on the dining room table, or else I had a school project there that I didn't want moved. In a way, the Thanksgiving table was an art project. The white tablecloth was topped with blue and white china, which was flanked with silver cutlery. Two crystal water glasses—twenty-four in all—stood by each plate. Toward the middle were several serving dishes and an assortment of tongs, big forks, and ladles, as well as four pewter candlesticks fitted with dark orange candles. In the very center, Mom had created an asymmetrical arrangement of gourds, Indian corn, acorns, walnuts, and greens that looked like it should be in a magazine. Mom must have thought so, too, because she had her camera out and was taking photos of it from all angles, in all kinds of different light.

"Want me to do the dishes?"

"You are an angel, Lexi. I should really wait until the food is on the table to photograph it, shouldn't I? But I suspect I will be too distracted tomorrow to remember my camera."

"Isn't that fork a little crooked?"

"Is it? You're right!" When Mom got out her ruler and started to measure the distance of each plate rim from the edge of the table, as though we lived in the

White House and were preparing for a State dinner, I knew it was time for me to quietly slip away into the relative calm of the kitchen. Luckily I knew Mom just had her pre-game jitters and would settle down soon.

By Thanksgiving morning, Mom was calm, Dad was peeling potatoes, and I was like a superheated molecule, zooming here and there with my video camera trying to capture all the textures, colors, and action. I only wished that I could have found a way to preserve the delicious smells and wonderful tastes of the food digitally. Probably some hot-shot Caltech or MIT grad has mastered that technology and next year it will be the number one Christmas gift. That day, though, I just had my eyes, ears, camera, keen nose, and over-active taste buds to fix the day in my memory.

Just when Mom's calm was starting to fray around the edges, Dad boomed out in his bass voice:

"Over the river and through the woods,
To Sundog, MINN we've come.
Thanksgiving means food, we're in the mood,
We're going to get us soooo-ome!"

That made us laugh. I put the camera aside and pulled an apron over my head. Mom's shoulders stopped migrating towards her ears. She hummed the tune as she placed the potatoes Dad had peeled and quartered into an enormous kettle of boiling salty water.

"Alexa," Mom said, "you can slice the bread. Then cover it so it doesn't dry out. Paul, if you'd just drain the potatoes and keep them in the warm kettle with the lid on? I'll mash them in a few minutes." She looked around. "I think we're good, and no guests arriving for fifteen minutes. I am going to freshen up."

She was so distracted that she didn't even notice my grubby sneakers or ratty grey Princeton hoodie with the orange and black Tigers insignia. But I was nothing if not a thoughtful daughter that day. I already had an outfit laid out upstairs, and it was *not my style*. It wasn't just a dress, it was a corduroy dress in rust, with long fitted sleeves, a high collar, fitted bodice, and long skirt. Mom had fallen in love with it and bought it for me the year before. It was expensive. I tried it on when it came, but it was too big and I simply refused to wear it, saying it made me feel like Nellie Oleson, that snooty shopkeeper's daughter who menaced Laura Ingalls Wilder. Mom didn't try to argue with me for once, but I saw her face kind of crumple. The dress had moved with us from New York, and I thought the color was just right for Thanksgiving. Also, I wanted to let Mom know how much I appreciated the effort she had put into this holiday (even if I had some mixed feelings about it).

"Dad," I said, dusting off my hands and covering the bread, "I need to freshen up, too."

"You green-eyed ladies are lovely in anything," he said with a wink, "but go ahead. Make yawsef gaawwgous!"

I went upstairs and took off my sweats and put on a pair of chocolate brown tights, then pulled the dress over my head. Luckily, the buttons were in the front. Since the buttonholes hadn't been used much, they were stiff. I put on my slouchy brown suede boots and then ran a comb through my red-gold hair. Last of all, I put on a headband that was covered with bright blue silk. Then I went back downstairs.

Mom was already in the dining room, striking a match. "Why, Alexa!" she said, sounding quite surprised. She stood still, then waved the lit match out. "You look... just beautiful!"

"Thanks," I mumbled, suddenly a bit shy. "So do you." She did, too, in a long black satin skirt and white blouse, with a brooch of cranberry-colored glass beads glinting between her collar bones.

"Thank you," she said. She came over and gave my shoulders a quick squeeze. "It's going to be a fun day. Really different." Then Mom nodded toward the candles. "Do you want to do the honors?"

"May I?"

"Certainly." She handed me the box of Diamond stick matches. I slid the cardboard drawer open, selected one, and closed the drawer. It took me a couple of tries, but at last I felt a little snap as the match head traveled across the sandpaper and the match flared to life. Quickly, I touched its tip to the white cotton wicks in the centers of the orange candles. The flames danced for a moment, then settled into lovely arcs of shimmering light.

At that moment, the doorbell rang. Mom jumped into action. I hurried to dispose of the burnt match. Then I joined Mom at the front door to welcome the Davenports.

"Hello," we all said.

"May I take your coats?" Mom asked, tactfully assisting Mrs. Davenport out of her heavy woolen outerwear. Mrs. Davenport was little and lively from the front, but from the side you could see that osteoporosis was settling in for a long stay. It was difficult for her to lift her arms. Mr. Davenport, who was older than she, slipped out of his black camel's hair topcoat with surprising grace. He reminded me of an otter gliding from dry land into the water. I got the feeling he liked parties.

I took their coats into the study and laid them on the leather settee. When I returned, the Davenports were seated in wing chairs and Dad was pouring them each a glass of amber-colored sherry.

The doorbell rang again. It was Ursula and her dad, Mike.

"Hey," I said to Ursula. She was wearing a red dress with long sleeves, simple and pretty. I had never seen her in a dress before, but I knew better than to mention that.

"Hey," she answered gruffly.

"Would you like some ginger ale?"

"Okay."

I led the way to the kitchen. Dad had placed a cut-glass champagne bucket on the counter and filled it with ice. A pair of chrome tongs rested on top like a frigid silver bird.

As I thunked the cubes in glasses and poured the fizzy soda, Ursula and I began to giggle for no reason.

"It smells good in here," Ursula said, sipping her bubbles.

"It should. We've been cooking things for days. Cooking, but not eating much. It's funny, but when you cook a lot the urge to eat goes away."

"That's hard."

"Tell me about it. Take-out pizza instead of ham and buttered biscuits and turkey and gravy and corn pudding…"

"Wow!" Ursula said. "Dad usually just grills a steak. Or else we go to the holiday buffet at a restaurant. Even if Mom weren't too busy, she doesn't like to cook, and Dad… I guess he doesn't know how."

"Let's go wait on the porch for Isabelle."

"Sure."

We carried our glasses to the front door. Mom was passing a plate of deviled eggs and capers. Dad was getting a drink for Mike. Ursula and I slipped out onto the porch. Cherryvale Street looked spare, even stark, without the golden-orange blaze of the maple leaves. The lone cherry tree, smack in the middle of our front lawn, was also leafless. Its knobby bark seemed to twist into a spiral around its trunk in a way that made me think of the turning of the year. Winter was a long time here, but when spring came around again it would look like a pinky-white cloud resting on an umbrella handle.

I knew, however, that Ursula would not be interested in these thoughts.

"So, how is your soccer team doing?" I asked her.

"Awesome! We've got a shot at the championship. Our goalie isn't such a sieve this year. Some of the kids can even pass the ball."

"That's great. If you win, do you go to a state tournament?"

"No. We're peewee. But in high school, yeah."

"Cool."

We fiddled with our ice. I started to feel cold, despite the unseasonably warm day. A dark green station wagon pulled up to the curb, and we saw Isabelle's face through the window. She waved vigorously. The instant the vehicle came to a complete stop, her door popped open and she shot out of the car, taking the steps so quickly that her feet were a blur.

"Your room," she hissed to me. "The twins are insane."

Ursula and I followed on her heels.

"Hi, everybody," Isabelle called politely on her way to the stairs.

"Be back in a bit," I added.

Ursula just giggled.

When we reached my room, we all entered in a tumble. I closed the door and locked it.

"You have *no* idea," said Isabelle, "what luxury you enjoy." She began pulling off the sleeves of her coat, continuing. "First of all, you are only children. And second, you have locks on your doors."

"Twins are kind of interesting, though," Ursula began, a teasing glint in her eye.

"Don't even start." Isabelle cut Ursula off with a slicing gesture of her left hand. "First of all, last week, the dreaded double birthday arrived. That is always a circus. Then, they each got a chemistry set. Chemistry! Aunt Rhoda doesn't understand that they are only six years old. Or else she thinks that they are little geniuses or something. And so this morning I found several things I had been missing, and more I didn't even know they'd taken, in a stash in their room. Those monsters cut swatches out of all my skirts to test the fiber content. They pulverized my pearl necklace to test the pH balance. And—this is the worst—they cut some of Molly's hair to look at it under the microscope!"

I gave a gasp of horror. Ursula looked blasé. I suspected it was just the kind of thing she would have done in her younger years. But I knew how special an American Girl doll was. I treasured my own Felicity doll. Molly, Isabelle's doll, was the brown-haired one with glasses from the 1940s. If she had had blonde hair, she would have looked just like Isabelle.

Isabelle looked at me and nodded fiercely. Her chin puckered until it looked like a peach pit. Tears brightened her blue eyes. "So count your blessings," she said. "No brothers."

There was a knock on the door. Then a second knock. "Belle, we want to play, too."

"Go away, Marshall."

"Mom said."

"Said what, Mason?"

"You have to let us play."

"Forget it."

I decided to play Tom Sawyer. I opened the door a crack, despite Isabelle's frantic head-shaking. "Hey, guys," I said.

They looked up at me, expectant and skittish as rabbits. Marshall was taller and blonder. Mason had a sprinkling of caramel-colored freckles across his nose.

"My dad told me that he is counting on you," I said.

Marshall's eyes narrowed. "What for?"

"To carve the turkey, of course. But I was worried that you guys were too little."

"We just had our birthday," protested Mason.

"Yeah, but you have to be pretty strong to hold down the bird with the carving forks."

Two skinny arms sprang into my face. I felt their nano-biceps with appropriate awe. "Not bad. Not bad. Maybe you are old enough. Go see if you can persuade him."

They rushed down the stairs. It's true there were sharp knives down there, but there were also at least five parents.

Ursula and I comforted Isabelle the best way we, as brotherless friends, could figure out how to do. We turned her attention to more interesting things.

Before too long, Mom called us to the table. We sat down. Mercifully, Isabelle's parents flanked the twins, containing them on one side of the table. They looked so angelic that it was hard to credit what hellions they could be. I sat on the other side, with Ursula to my left and Isabelle on my right. Mike sat on Ursula's left. Mom sat with Mr. Davenport at one end of the table and Dad sat with Mrs. Davenport at the other end.

Mrs. Davenport turned to Dad and said, "Paul, if it's all right, may I offer an ecumenical blessing?"

"Please do," he replied.

She asked us to hold hands, and then, after looking at the golden candle flames for a moment, she said:

"Behold the bounty of the earth,
Here in this circle of friends.
May it sustain us,
In loving thoughts and wise actions."

"Hear, hear," we all said at once.

Mr. Davenport cleared his throat, then observed, in his deep voice, "Viola, dear, that far outstrips ecumenical. It's positively and beautifully deist."

"Thank you, Rufus. I seek to please but not offend any and all forms of the godhead, whether dominant or dormant."

After that, conversation turned to the food and how to keep all of the dishes circulating. Dad jumped up to pour champagne for the adults, while Mom offered sparkling white grape juice to us kids.

I took a bite of turkey and secretly put it into my napkin. Chalk it up to Mom. Right again. I loved the gorgonzola and walnuts, but meat does repel me at some cellular level. I was just going to have to face the fact that I was designed to be a vegetarian, maybe even a vegan.

"I see we are twelve," remarked Mr. Davenport.

"Yes," said Mom. "Thank goodness for Aunt Margie's wedding china. And the table and chairs, of course. Those old sets were made in the days of big families, and they were always for twelve. Now everything comes in sets of four everywhere—eight, if you're lucky."

"Maybe the sets of twelve were to plan ahead for the usual cracks and chips," suggested Frances Porter, Isabelle's mom.

"Lots of that in the E.R., eh, Frances," said Isabelle's dad, Kevin.

"Yes, but even with glue, china doesn't really mend. The human body is amazingly resilient."

Mr. Davenport coughed delicately. "When I see twelve at table, I think of the amazing resilience of the

Divine. As Joseph Campbell had it, the 'masks of eternity.'"

"Do you mean the twelve Olympians?" I asked.

"In part." He beamed at me. "Certainly the Greek pantheon springs to mind. Does anyone think of others?"

"Eskimos!" shouted the twins together.

Mr. looked momentarily nonplussed. Each twin had a Porter parent turn to hush him.

Isabelle spoke up. "Please don't mind them. Eskimos are all they think about. They are planning to build an igloo if we ever get any snow."

"A snow yurt," said Ursula, then added under her breath, "for teeny-tiny nerds."

Isabelle and I snorted with choked laughter. I recovered as quickly as I could, because I wanted to help Mr. Davenport along. Sometimes he took a while to get there, but he usually arrived at an interesting point.

"Are you thinking of Norse mythology?"

Mr. Davenport rubbed his hands and shot a grateful glance to me. I dug into my mashed potatoes and listened with one ear as he talked about the Norse pantheon.

"The *Prose Edda* is quite interesting, as a matter of fact. Not twelve, but twelve plus one. It specifies that there were twelve seats for the gods and a high seat—a throne—for Odin."

"Sounds like the Last Supper," offered Dad. "Twelve disciples and Jesus."

"There are some similarities, though not close ones," nodded Mr. Davenport.

"Tell about Loki," I asked, and he happily obliged, explaining the sad story of how blind Hod was tricked into killing his gentle brother Baldur by Loki with an arrow of mistletoe wood.

"I have never understood this story," I confessed. "I just don't get it. First, why did Loki have it in for Baldur—and Hod, too, because he had to forfeit his own life? But then Loki was punished anyway. Why did Hod have to die if Loki was guilty?"

"Loki is an unsettling figure. There is in him the free-floating evil and cunning of Iago, a love of conflict for its own sake. But there is a larger question, too, of community culpability, I think. The Aesir had a history of profiting from trickery and broken faith. Perhaps Loki only extends the magnitude of their double-dealing and turns it back upon them."

"Like a mirror?" suggested Isabelle.

"Or a laser, perhaps?" offered Frances.

"Interesting thought, that. I seem to recall a very good volume on this subject..."

Just then Mike's cell phone rang. "Sorry," he said, looking at the display. "It's from Danielle."

I looked at Ursula, remembering Danielle was her mother's name. She didn't look at me but down at her plate, scowling.

Mike continued, "I should take it. Please excuse me for a moment." He stood and walked into the living room.

Mom stood and signaled to me with her eyes. I popped up, too. "May I take your plates?" I said to Isabelle and Ursula.

"We'll help!" they said.

Before Mike returned, looking annoyed, we had the table cleared, and Dad had pressed the button on the coffee maker. Mom and Frances had started dishing out desert.

"Everything okay?" asked Mom.

"It's nothing major," said Mike. "Ursula, your mom has a wild hair..." He stopped, remembering where he was. "That is, your mother called to ask if plans could change. She would like to pick you up today instead of tomorrow morning. Actually, now."

Ursula sat with her red sleeves crossed over her chest. "So I don't even get a choice, do I?"

Mike walked over and put his hand on her shoulder.

She shrugged it off.

"I can call her back and tell her the whole weekend is off!" Mike looked a little guilty.

"You can't. *A Christmas Carol* opens tomorrow. And it's tech week for that Genet play in the Lab," Ursula countered.

Mom put down the pie and cleared her throat. "Ursula, I'm sure you'll have a good time with your

146

mother. But if you need a Plan B during the weekend, you can always stay with us."

Ursula looked at Mom with pink-rimmed eyes. She didn't cry, though. "Thank you," she said simply. Then she turned to her dad. "It's okay," she said.

The doorbell rang. Ursula stood up, knowing it would be her mom at the door. "I'll get my coat," she said and marched off like a little wooden soldier.

Mike opened the door. Danielle breezed past him, flipping her mobile phone shut, as she slid her enormous sunglasses up onto the top of her head, where they perched like a raven on her long, curly, red hair. Her gold bracelets jangled as she slipped the cell phone into the pocket of her leopard-print coat. From where I sat, I could smell her perfume, strong and insinuating.

"Hi, everyone." Her berry-colored lips curved up, but her eyes narrowed. "What did I miss?"

No one else spoke for a minute. Danielle didn't repeat her question. Ursula came around the corner. "Are you ready, love?" asked her mother.

Ursula raised her eyebrows at her mother, then turned away with all the languid contempt of a silent film star. "Thank you for a lovely dinner," she said in the direction of my parents. Ignoring her father, she brushed past her mother onto the porch.

Danielle shrugged, smiled another grimace, and said, "See you Sunday," to Mike. Then she turned and pulled the door closed behind her as she exited.

THE HOWLING VOWELS

Not knowing what else to do, I put a forkful of pie in my mouth. I felt sad. I felt unsettled. I felt very happy that my mom and dad lived in the same house.

Chapter Eleven
"Happy Holidays"

It was a frosty Friday night deep in December. We stepped out onto the porch. Dad had shoveled the snow into white mounds that lined both sides of the front walk and sparkled where the yellow light from the streetlamp touched it. The air was frosty, and the sky was a color I never saw in the city. It was a deep refreshing blue. White stars glinted as though they were shards of ice sprinkled across the bottom of a vast cobalt glass bowl.

All of us were warmly dressed. We made a visual symphony of Gore-Tex, fleece, and colorful wool. Otto's father, Vernon, led us from house to house. We sang "Jingle Bells," "It Came upon a Midnight Clear," and "Walking in a Winter Wonderland." Every door, it seemed, was decorated with fragrant greens and shiny red ribbons. Everyone invited us in, but we politely declined because we weren't even cold. Mrs. Davenport was especially insistent, so while we obliged her with an encore, Mr. Davenport brought out paper cups and a thermos of cocoa.

With our stomachs warmed, it seemed as if the songs and the frosty air were making us seem to float with holiday feeling. We didn't even want to talk. Between houses, we kept so silent that we could hear the new snow squeak under our boot soles like cornstarch. Okay, maybe that is not the most poetic image, but it truly sounded and looked like that. And our singing was really pretty good. Never had the Howling Vowels been more melodious, in my opinion.

After nearly an hour of winding our way around the neighborhood and singing, Vernon said, "Anyone else thinking about hot gingerbread and whipped cream?"

"Me!" we all shouted.

He chuckled in his baritone way. "I guess we don't need a recount. Just one more stop, and we'll head on back to our place."

We had come to the faded little red house opposite the park. The windows were dark, and the door was unadorned.

"Um, Dad,' said Otto. "I don't think anyone is at home."

Vernon led us up the curving path, unshoveled though it was. "Let's see," he said. He reached the porch ahead of us and leaned in to ring the bell. "Ho, ho, ho, Miss Arnold. Merry Christmas!"

Faster than I expected, the porch light snapped on—just a naked bulb hanging near the doorframe. I looked at Iz. Her eyes got even more round than usual.

"Who's there?" A high and suspicious voice asked from a small gap between the door and the doorframe. A tarnished chain prevented it from opening further.

"It's Vernon Bell, from down the street. These are my children, Otto and Zinny. And these are their friends, Isabelle, Eduardo, Alexa, and Ursula."

"Oh. Well, what do you want?"

"It is such a pretty night that we are out caroling. We'd like to sing for you, if we may."

There was a long silence. It made me uncomfortable. Then the voice said, "Just a minute," and the door closed.

Vernon turned to us. "Miss Arnold wasn't expecting company," he said.

Talk about stating the obvious!

"She..." Before he could finish, the inner door burst open. A small round lady stood in the doorframe. She was wearing the shaggiest boots I had ever seen, a shiny down-filled coat, mittens that had holes in the thumbs, two knitted scarves, and a man's wool driving cap. At the sides of the cap, her short white hair stood out like straw. Behind her wire-rimmed glasses, her brown eyes appeared huge, startled, and watchful. Altogether she reminded me of an owl.

"Okay. I'm out here for this snowy-season tricky-treat thing. Shoot."

I wanted to go right home. I think we all did. Sometimes good deeds just blow up in your face. But, she was a neighbor, even if she was an old and cranky one. So, with a glance at Otto and Isabelle, Eddie and Ursula, we sang *Silver Bells*. Maybe it was my imagination, but I thought I saw her face soften a little. She didn't quite smile, though. But it was enough to make me braver.

"Miss Arnold?"

"Hmmm?"

"Do you have a favorite carol?"

She closed one eye and cleared her throat. "Well, now that you mention it... I always used to like *Rudolph the Red-Nosed Reindeer*."

"We know that one, don't we, kids?" Vernon winked at us, and we began together.

At the conclusion of the song, Miss Arnold blew her nose. "Can't stand out here all night. Can't let you go away empty-handed, neither. Wait here." The storm door banged shut behind her as she popped back into her house for a moment. "Just a minute, just a minute," she called faintly from deep inside. Then she popped out again. She thrust her mittened hands at us with a startling crackle. "Here!"

I saw even Ursula flinch a little.

But Vernon was saying, "How kind, ma'am. We do appreciate it," as he tore a cellophane covered candy cane off of a long roll.

We all followed suit, saying, "Thank you," as we tore off what seemed like Christmas tickets.

"Everybody got one? Well, okay then. I don't know how old these are, had 'em a long time. But they're wrapped. Good night, then."

Miss Arnold turned her back and took one step toward the door. Then she stopped and turned.

"Oh," she said. "Merry Christmas." And then she hurried inside.

Ursula had stayed over the night before because her parents were both out of town. Her mom was in a play in New York, so she was going to be gone for six months if the play did well, maybe longer. And her dad, Mike, was in Seattle, but just for the weekend.

We both slept in a little, but I woke up first. I poked Ursula in the ribs.

"Hey, Ursula! You're snoring like a bear. Wake up."

Ursula groaned and turned over. "You're snoring like a dragon."

"No way!"

"Oh, way."

"Do you think Miss Arnold snores?"

We both burst into giggles for some reason.

"Those candy canes were a hundred years old," Ursula said.

"Yeah. Musty. But she seemed kind of nice, though. She really likes Rudolph. A person can't be bad if she likes Rudolph. But," I continued, hesitantly, "do you think she has many friends?"

"It doesn't seem like it."

"That's too bad. I am glad Otto's dad had us stop."

"Yeah." Ursula turned to one side and leaned her head on her hand. "Man, that sure was good gingerbread."

"Wasn't it? I could have some right now."

"Me, too! What's for breakfast?"

"Let's go find out."

An hour later, Mom, Dad, Ursula, and I were all in the mini-van on our way to a local tree farm. I had never been to such a place.

"Dad?"

"Mm-hmm."

"You know how we always got our Christmas tree from a lot in the city?"

"Yep."

"Well, I thought they were cut in the forest. In the deep forests of Maine or Canada, maybe. I never thought about having farms for trees."

"Well, Lexi there are probably farms for everything that grows. You know, catfish farms, orange groves, strawberry fields. Oh! Remember that industrial stretch around Gary, Indiana?"

"Sure I do. I wish I didn't."

"That's called a 'tank farm.'" Dad chuckled. "Oh, and I've read that people who use computers all day in a routine way for their jobs are said to work on 'electronic plantations.'"

"That's awful!" said Ursula. "It sounds like slavery."

"Some people do call it 'wage slavery,'" Dad agreed. "I don't, though. It's nothing like the Athenian silver mines at Laurium where life expectancy was about a minute and a half. It's not even as bad as walking the soybean fields like I had to do as a boy."

"What are you, then?" I asked, knowing that my dad worked on his computer all day.

"I would like to think of myself as a 'symbolic analyst.' Doesn't that sound more impressive than 'wage ape?'"

We all giggled.

"Still," he stretched his arm out and squeezed Mom's shoulder. "It feels good to have a few days off."

"It's good to see you so happy, Paul. You have been working a lot of hours, though."

"I won't do any more billable hours until next year, then."

I thought about how in the big city, Dad used to return from the subway looking slow and tired. Now I loved how he would step out of his office at home, close the door, and say, "How's that for a commute," as he whistled his way into the kitchen.

"That's right! Pretty soon it will be 2010," said Mom.

I was thinking that when March rolled around again we will have been in Sundog for a whole year without even a visit yet to New York. I wanted to visit again someday, but I wasn't missing it as much as before. Then I had another thought. "You know what is really cool, Ursula? You, me, Otto, all the Howling Vowels, we are turn of the century kids *and* turn of the millennium kids, because we were all born in 1999."

"Wow! I never thought about that."

"I know. Me, neither. But think about it. Except for those born with us, no one will have that for a thousand years."

"Oh! There it is, Paul," said Mom as she pointed to the left.

We turned off the county road and onto a gravel driveway. There was a shed with cut trees leaning against the walls, and a cashier's area. All around, as far as we could see, were gentle slopes covered with soft snow and the dark green triangles of Christmas trees. Some were tiny, some were medium-sized, and some were huge.

Dad talked a minute with one of the employees. Then he came back to us. "Okay," he said, as he handed Mom and me each a red plastic tie with our name 'Stevens' written on it in ink, "here's the deal: it's like a treasure hunt. We're looking for a tree that looks good from all sides and is no more than 8 feet high.

Everybody, hold up your right hand, as high as you can. That's right. Now, the tree can be a little bit higher than your highest reach. Otherwise, it won't fit in the living room with the star on top. We'll go off in teams and meet back here in, say," he looked at his watch, "twenty minutes. Any questions?"

We all shook our heads.

"Go!"

Ursula and I bounded like snowshoe rabbits through the powdery drifts. It was fun walking through the quiet avenues of trees. It was hard choosing. Every tree looked perfect at first glance, but as we looked closer we saw the flaws. This one had a big gap in the branches up high, while that one had a crooked trunk.

Finally, Ursula spotted a straight tree with even branches that we both thought looked just right.

"Mmmmmm," I said putting my nose right up against the needles. "This smells so good."

"Yeah," Ursula agreed. She was quiet for a moment, then said, "We have a metal tree."

"You do?"

She nodded. "Mom got it a few years ago. It is from the 1940s, still in its original box. It's made of silver tinsel, I think. You put it together like you do tent poles. It is really shiny, but there is no smell."

"Will you have your mom for Christmas here? Or go up to her place?"

Ursula kicked up some of the snow in a dusty spray. "Who knows? I mean, she says she's having me with her in New York for three days, that we'll go skating in Rockefeller Plaza and see the gigantic tree there. But she hasn't sent the tickets yet." Ursula blinked hard. "I bet it will be like last year. Dad and I will just put up the metal tree the night before and make toaster waffles with syrup on Christmas morning. Open a few gifts or whatever and play video games until it gets dark."

I knew that Mike loved video games, even more than most kids, and I remembered how unhappy Ursula had seemed at Thanksgiving when her mom came to get her. I had been meaning to ask her about it, but with one thing and another there just had not been a good moment. I didn't know if she even wanted to talk, but I had never heard her say so much at one time. So I said, "It must be hard having your parents split up."

"It's not great. But at least they don't fight. As much. Not in the same room, anyway."

"That's rugged." I gave her a squeeze around the shoulders, like Mom does to me. Ursula stood very still but she didn't jump away.

"Look," I said, to change the subject. I pointed to a nest in a nearby tree.

"Cool," said Ursula.

We walked quietly closer.

"I think it is a blackbird's nest," Ursula said. "See how it is woven into a cup shape at the bottom?"

"There's nobody home now, is there?"

160

Ursula gave me her one-sided smile. "Nope. They migrate."

"Good. I wouldn't want to freak anybody out."

We both turned then to the sound of Dad's voice calling our names. We had lost track of time. There he was at the end of the row, small against the evergreens in his red and black checked jacket.

"We're here! We're here!" we called as we jumped high and waved our hands. "We found something perfect."

Three weeks later, after the Christmas decorations were repacked for next year, the tree was on the curb, and the last of the fragrant balsam fir needles were swept up, I was starting in with my usual routines. I was struggling a little with Norwegian prepositions, but I was determined to master them so I would have an easier time with Old English and Icelandic. I was also diving into the pre-algebra I had been putting off during the holidays, as well as piano and Minnesota history and geography.

Sometimes my friends who go to public school think homeschoolers just sleep late and play video games every day. Maybe some do. And hey, you can learn a lot from games. But I like to study interesting things with a little more structure. It's just what works for me. And some day I am going to read all the Norse myths in their original forms!

Anyway, I remembered it was on January 6th that the best gift of the whole season landed in the mailbox. Epiphany—the day when the Wise Men found the stable—is part of the Christmas story but it had never meant anything to me. But that Epiphany was the day that Señor Raoul sent a response to our Christmas letter that contained an invitation for me.

Mom was in her studio, and Dad was in his office when the mail arrived; so I brought it all in and divided it into four piles: Mom, Dad, me, and junk. The thick envelope from the Raouls was addressed to us all so I decided not to wait to open it.

There was a folded letter, some pictures of Señor and Señora with their children, Maria and Luis, and something else, a printed e-mail with something written in pen on the margin. The handwriting said, "We were glad to learn of Alexa's new interest in video production. Luis received this notice from one of his professors at NYU. Would Alexa be interested in applying?"

Hmmmm. What could it be?

I read more closely. It was an announcement for the first annual Young Filmmakers Competition. The deadline was in a few weeks.

You know what? I didn't hesitate even a moment. Pre-algebra could wait! This was exactly what I wanted to do next, and it would take everything I had to put a good entry together.

I pulled out the camera manual and turned on the computer. I would have to get a lot better with the editing software. I would need to shoot more footage. But I had an idea, and I just fell into it headlong.

Chapter Twelve
"Ice Sculptures and Caves"

It was the month of hearts and flowers, but you'd never know it in Sundog. For a whole week I hadn't seen one chunk of blue sky, not a single teeny-tiny sliver. It seemed too cold to snow—twenty below zero at night—but not, apparently, too cold for the wind to blow.

Ever since I'd gotten up this morning, I'd felt chilled and edgy. The deadline for the NYU Young Filmmakers contest was at the end of the week. The film was ready. It was the best I could make it. But I hadn't told anyone except Mom and Dad. Also, I was just plain stumped over the application forms.

Now I was taking a break, just gazing at the painting on the other side of the dining room over Mom's left shoulder, the humorous one she'd made of a red dog, an orange sun, a green house all composed on a dark green field.

"What are you staring at?" Mom asked.

When I didn't answer, she nodded sagely. "Ah. Of course. It's my immortal beauty, again, casting its usual spell."

She didn't appear to notice when I snorted.

Mom's show at the Sundog Art Center was coming up soon. All the canvases were complete. Since she liked raw edges, nothing was matted or framed. Mom fretted over this a little, not knowing if the local audience would see that as amateur or sloppy, since the work she'd seen here was all neatly bordered and framed. Then Dad suggested that she draft an artist statement that explained her aesthetic, so now she was kind of tearing her hair out over the computer. That is, when she wasn't making over-the-top statements in my direction.

I went over and leaned up against her. "I think we're in the same boat, Mom."

"How's that?"

"This application is driving me bananas. Just the sight of these little boxes makes me break out into a cold sweat, even when they ask for something I know, like my address. But when they ask for a synopsis of the plot or this... what does 'Summarize your vision as a director relative to today's youth' mean? I just freeze."

Mom sighed and looked into my eyes. Slowly she nodded. "You're right," she said.

"I am?"

"Yep." She put one of her hands on my forehead and the other on her own.

I felt one corner of my mouth tug up toward a smile.

"Yes. Just as I thought. We've both come down with a virulent case of cabin fever. Complicated by severe writer's block." She cocked an eyebrow at me. "You know vat zis means, don't you?" Her accent sounded vaguely Viennese.

I shook my head.

"There is only one cure. And it is truly extreme. Get your coat."

"Why? Where are we going?"

"To the Mall of America, of course. We're going to ride all the scariest rides, scream like little girls, and eat ice cream under the dusty ficus trees. That will shake loose these writer's block shackles."

As we headed north we passed field after field of glazed and frozen snow punctuated here and there with the brown trunks of deciduous trees and the pyramidal green-black shapes of the conifers. Every so often, the rectilinear forms of farmhouses, barns, and sheds rose out of the land. There was a timeless, storybook quality to the landscape, as though we had fallen headfirst into the pages of a picture book.

After fifteen or twenty miles, though, we passed a large greenhouse on the left—shuttered for the season —and bright orange gates of the Lao Buddhist temple on the right, next to a little airport, and just beyond, a massive car dealership. We were in Lakeville or Apple Valley, one of the southern suburbs of the Twin Cities.

Before too long, we were part of a river of vehicles streaming toward the distant towers of the metropolis. Mom popped one of her favorite CDs into the CD player, and after we had heard the whole title cut three times, we were gliding our midnight blue Saturn sedan with the "Don't Be So Lopsided" bumper sticker onto the Hawaiian Pineapple level of the Mall of America parking lot.

By then I was giggling over nothing. My bad mood had evaporated, and I was ready to tackle the log flume ride or even the two-story-high Thor's hammer ride, as well as hot dogs, ice cream cones, and pizza. I was even ready to sit with Mom while she had a complete makeover at the Nordstrom's makeup counter. The makeup consultant used ten different products and six different brushes on Mom. When she was done, Mom turned around and asked "What do you think, Alexa?"

"Well," I said truthfully, "I don't see that much makeup. You look just like you, only a little smoother and brighter."

"Great!" said Mom. "Just the look I was going for." She bought a new lipstick called "Goddess Glow," a rosy-brown color.

"What about all the rest of that stuff?" I asked.

"Maybe another time," said Mom. "Right now, I feel a splendid idea coming on." She took my hand and gave me that Mom-of-Mystery look, guiding me back

168

into the main flow of pedestrians streaming in and out of shops.

"Where are we going?" I asked.

"We're almost there," she responded.

And then there we were indeed, in front of the new American Girl Store, two stories high, shining like Oz did to Dorothy. I didn't even wait for Mom but skipped inside. Then I stopped. I had never imagined so many beautiful dolls, clothes, and accessories in one place. It was like a museum but better because these things could possibly come home and be your own forever.

Mom smiled at the look on my face. I still wasn't moving, so she tugged my sleeve and said, "Look over here, A."

I walked beside her, stumbling a little because I was trying to look in all directions at once. Just ahead, I saw where Mom was going, toward the historical dolls. She stopped right in front of the Kirsten display.

The Kirsten books had always been among my favorites, and since I had moved to Minnesota I had reread them because I felt a little like her, a pioneer in a prairie state. But I had never seen the doll for real before, only looking back at me from the catalog pages. Here she was. Mom was still talking but I wasn't listening, just looking hard.

"Earth to Alexa," said Mom, waving her hand in front of my eyes.

"Isn't she beautiful?"

"Yes," Mom said softly. "Would you like to…"

I was instantly alert. "What?"

"Take her home?"

"Really?"

Mom nodded. I hugged her hard. She laughed. I just couldn't believe it because Mom is not at all extravagant when it comes to buying toys, and I already had Felicity.

"I noticed you've been rereading the Kirsten series. You both adjusted well to life in Minnesota."

The next few moments were a delightful blur. I couldn't wait to tell Isabelle. I knew she would have great ideas for making new doll clothes out of scraps and broken jewelry. Before long, Mom, Kirsten, and I were all in the car, each one of us wearing mittens and wooly hats, flying past the snowy fields toward Sundog.

By the time we returned home, we both felt a lot better. Mom claimed the laptop. I decided to take a walk with my camera before the sun completely left the sky. The wind had stopped blowing and the western edge of the horizon was pink and orange. The ideas flowed inside me so thick and fast that I no longer felt the cold. I walked over to the Birchwood campus, crossing the crusty snow by the side door of the gothic chapel. In the evening light, the ice sculptures carved by students for their winter carnival looked warm and alive. I stood for a while between a translucent bust of Elvis and a gigantic Stratocaster guitar, examining them each in turn. Then I found my favorite, a penguin with clear wings and an icicle for a beak.

While I filmed the pink and gold sunset as it reflected in the ice carvings, I started thinking about my next film. I would bring Norse myth to new life, filming appropriate sites throughout this winter and into the year, using whatever quirky props I could find. It was very exciting to think of making a Trollheim in the woods. How would I create Aasgaard, and the rainbow bridge to the gods? Maybe Professor Davenport would have an idea. I would rewrite the myths for voice over, and…

My thoughts swirled with pleasure.

As I thought about the new film, suddenly I knew what I wanted to say about my first one. I wanted to say to everyone that I like fantasy books as much as the next person, but that I am also drawn to all the magic that underlies the stuff of daily life, if only we have eyes to see it. And that I think that is the real gift of fantasy, mythology, religion—call it what you like. Those golden frames allow us to see the glory and enchantment present in our own lives.

And then, suddenly, I was hungry and thirsty. I turned off the camera and sped toward home, crunching across the twilit frozen snow like giants were chasing me. When I burst in the front door, Mom looked up, first startled, then amused.

"Goodness, Alexa! It is like the north wind blew you in."

"I'm starving."

Mom saved her file and stood up from the dining room table. "You hang up your things. I will get you a snack."

As I pulled off my boots, she leaned back through the kitchen door to remark, "You must have had a breakthrough. I always get hungry when the creative juices are flowing."

"Right and right. But first things first. May I have some hot chocolate and cinnamon toast?"

"Absolutely."

A few moments later, I was licking the sugar from my fingers with a warm feeling in my belly. Outside it was growing dark, but inside it was cozy and light. Mom said that I could have the laptop all evening, if I needed it. But I thought half an hour would be plenty of time. For once, I knew just what to say and how to say it.

Chapter Thirteen
"The End: or, Loop de Loop!"

Thirteen is my favorite number. It's a prime, of course. Which means it is just itself. Thirteen is the basis for the lunar calendar. Kids transform into teenagers on their thirteenth birthdays. When it masquerades as a baker's dozen, it means a little something extra. It is a mysterious number, but it is not dangerous. I am always surprised when people are afraid of it, because it is not spooky but lucky. Like June 13th, when we got to take part in the benefit show for the library.

That's why, on April 13th, I was half expecting something interesting to happen, but I didn't know what, and I didn't know when. After lunch, I was pounding out my own knock-off song, "Iron Girl," on the Baldwin near the door. When the doorbell blatted, I just about jumped through my skin. Mom was upstairs, so I answered the door. Mr. Reynolds, the mail carrier, handed me a long white package with red and blue trim, and asked me to sign for it. Boy, was I glad that I had been practicing cursive! I loved how the "x" in my first name looked clear and strong.

It had my name on it, so I could have just opened it, but when I saw the return address was NYU I got a little weak in the knees. They were probably returning my DVD. Even without opening it, I could just guess what the letter said:

> Dear Alexa Stephens,
> We regret to inform you, Yada yada yada, here's your sub-par entry back, loser.
> Sincerely, The Judges

I was really glad I hadn't told the other kids anything. It was hard, because I am not good at keeping secrets, but now I could see the value of it.

Mom walked into the dining room. "Hi, honey. Did I hear the doorbell?"

I nodded. "Mr. Reynolds with the mail."

"Anything interesting?"

"Nope. Well…" I waved one corner of the long white envelope. "My DVD came back."

Mom came over and gave me a hug. "I am proud of you for giving it a try, Alexa."

"Thanks, Mom."

"You know, it was your first film. They must have had entries from all over the country. The main thing is that you had a vision and you went for it."

"I guess."

"Did they give you any kind of feedback?"

"No." I flapped the cardboard envelope against my leg. "I mean, I didn't really look yet."

Mom took the envelope from my hand. "Honey, you didn't even open it." She looked at me with that searching look she gets. "Do you mind if I do?"

I shook my head. "Go ahead."

Mom pulled the zipper tab and shook the contents onto the dining room table. No DVD, but two letters. One for me, on the school letterhead, and one from a lawyer. She glanced at the letters, then put her glasses on and read them thoroughly. You would think I would have been dancing around, but I just couldn't move. Finally, Mom pushed her glasses up on the top of her head and held the first letter out to me. "Here, Lexi," she said. "You should read this."

I took it from her. I could feel my forehead wrinkling a little. I looked up at Mom incredulously. She was smiling and nodding. "Does this really say what I think it does?"

"Congratulations! *You won!*" She took my hands and we jumped up and down like we were both little kids playing ring-around-the-rosy. I swear I could almost see Loki, the trickster god, nodding his shaggy head full of wild red hair. For once when the joke was on me, I couldn't have been more pleased.

177

The next few hours went by like one heartbeat. First, I had to read the second letter which was all about permissions from Mom and Dad for me to travel, etc. Then, I called up everybody. First Dad, of course, and then all the Howling Vowels. None of them could believe it. They all came over that evening, with their parents, for a screening. I don't think we had ever had so many people squeezed into our family room. To tell you the truth, I was pretty nervous. *What if they didn't like it? What if they told me I couldn't show it to strangers? What if they told me that I had betrayed their friendship and they never wanted to see me again?*

I bet even Charlie Chaplin at the opening of *The Little Tramp* was not as nervous as I was. He just had to please a studio. I had to please my family and friends and all of their families.

As the title sequence flashed *Everyday Magic* over the montage of our gang, people seemed happy. Then, with that first close-up of Isabelle, winking with one blue eye through her shining specs, everybody laughed in delight, including Isabelle. I think I must have held my breath for the whole twelve minutes, because when the applause came as the credits rolled, I let out a big *whoooosh* of a sigh.

"Cool," said Otto as he jigged in place. "We're movie stars."

"It's really funny, Alexa," said Isabelle with a sweet smile.

"*Magnifico!*" said Eduardo.

"Pretty wild, dude," said Ursula, giving me the high five.

Since then, it's been pretty busy. Otto and Ursula have gotten special permission to miss a few days of school. The local newspaper, the *Sundog Chronicle and Shopper*, did a story on local filmmakers and interviewed me. One old lady saw me on the street and said, "Hi, Alexa. Where's your camera?" I didn't even know her! The mayor of Sundog, Dave Ottoway, who also runs the local hardware store, saw me when I was buying some potting soil with my dad. Mayor Ottoway came over and shook my hand and said I was bringing honor to my hometown.

And that made me realize that, though I still miss New York sometimes, this really is home now. How funny that it would take strangers in New York City to make me realize it.

On May Day, I will be at Radio City Music Hall sharing ginger ale with the mayor of NYC. *Can you believe it?* My film will be shown for the first time on the silver screen. The big newspapers will be there. And the best part is that I will be back in New York City, but I won't be alone. Ursula, Otto, Eduardo, and Isabelle will be there, too.

And guess what?

Yep.

I bet we'll be howling!

THE END

ALEXA'S LEXICON

A Glossary of Words and Ideas
That Spark Her Imagination
by Julia Braulick

A

Asgaard [AZ-gard]; in Norse mythology, the paradise for warriors killed in battle and the home of the ruling Aesir gods

a cappella [ah-ca-PEL-a]; without instrumental sound (referring to singing)

aesthetic [es-THET-ik];dealing with artistic effect or beauty

alchemist [AL-kem-ist]; a person who practices alchemy, an early form of chemistry with philosophical and magical associations

Alexa [a-LEX-a]; a name meaning "noble" or "protector"

amateur [AM-a-cher]; a person who takes part in an activity for sheer enjoyment, not as a profession

amphitheater [AM-fuh-thee-a-ter]; a place for sporting events, contests, or spectacles, arranged so that the audience encircles the action

application [ap-li-KAY-shun]; a formal request, usually written, to enter a contest, school, or program

archaeopteryx [ar-key-OP-ter-iks]; the most primitive bird; lizardlike; lived with the biggest dinosaurs in the Jurassic Period

astigmatism [a-STIG-ma-tis-um]; impaired eyesight usually resulting from an irregularly shaped cornea and causing blurry vision

asymmetrical [ay-sim-MET-ri-kal]; without symmetry; unbalanced in appearance or structure

B

Baldur [BAL-door]; in Norse mythology, the god of light, beauty, and happiness; Loki tricked Hod into killing Baldur

Baldwin [BALD-win]; a piano made by the famous Baldwin Piano Company

banzai [BAHN-zy]; a Japanese cheer of triumph

barbershop quartet [BAR-ber-shop kwor-TET]; an unaccompanied quartet of voices singing in four-part harmony

Barcelona [bar-se-LONE-a]; the second largest city in Spain; the capital of Catalonia

baritone [BARE-i-tone]; the most common male voice type, lying between the bass and tenor voices; also called barytone

barium [BARE-ee-um]; a soft silvery-white metallic element

bass [BASE]; a singing voice of the lowest range

bell curve [BEL kurv] (or bell curve grading); a method of plotting the results of a class or a group to determine academic grades

benefit show [BEN-i-fit sho] (or benefit concert); a concert, show, or gala that is held to raise money for a good cause

binary [BY-na-ree]; a numbering system that uses only two digits (usually 0 and 1)

biography [by-OG-ra-fee]; an account of a person's life created by someone else

birch [BIRCH]; one tree of the genus Betula with papery bark and simple leaves, common in many northern forests

Blarney Stone [BLAR-nee stone]; a bluestone block set into Blarney Castle in Ireland; according to legend, anyone who kisses the stone will have great eloquence, or ability to convince people with words

Block Island [BLOCK AI-land]; an island in the Atlantic Ocean off the coast of Rhode Island

blasé [bla-ZAY]; bored or jaded with something because it is too familiar to be exciting

Bonnie and Clyde [BON-ee and CLIDE]; bank robbers who created a crime wave in the middle west and southern United States in the early 1930s; the band that Alexa hears perform is comprised of one female singer whose name is Bonnie and two guitarists who are known as "the Clydes" but really have other names

bounty [BOWN-tee]; generosity in giving, or a reward for capturing a criminal

boyo [BOY-o]; informal way of saying "boy" or "young man" in Wales or Ireland

brooch [BROCHE]; a decorative pin or clasp

Bunyan, Paul [BUN-yun, POL]; an imaginary giant lumberjack who is the hero of tall tales of the American Midwest; particularly associated with Minnesota

C

Caltech [KAL-tek]; California Institute of Technology, well known for engineering and science

Campbell, **Joseph** [KAM-bul, JOH-sef] (1904 to 1987); mythologist, writer, and lecturer

cannoli [ka-NO-lee]; yummy pastry dessert from Sicily; hard pastry shells filled with a soft, creamy, and sweet ricotta cheese filling

canvas [KAN-vis]; an extremely heavy-duty fabric; among many uses, it is stretched tight on wooden strips for use by artistic painters

Carnegie, Andrew [kar-NEG-ee, AN-droo] (1835 to 1919); American industrialist who donated millions of dollars for public libraries throughout the United States

Carroll, Lewis [KARE-ul, LOO-is] (1832 to 1898); the pen name of English author and mathematician Charles Lutwidge Dodgson; among his most famous writings are *Alice's Adventures in Wonderland*, its sequel *Through the Looking-Glass*, and the poem, "Jabberwocky"

catfish [KAT-fish]; a group of fish that have long bristly growths around their mouths, called barbels, that look and function like cats' whiskers to help them navigate in muddy river bottoms

cell [SEL]; the basic unit of life; humans have about 100 trillion

cellophane [SEL-a-fane]; a thin, transparent cellulose material made from wood pulp and used as wrapping

cephalothorax [sef-a-lo-THOR-aks]; the term used for the first (anterior) body section of arachnids and crustaceans; in these animals, the head and first body section are fused into one unit

Chagall, Marc [sha-GAL, MARK] (1887 to 1985); a Russian artist who worked in France

chaperon or **chaperone** [SHAP-er-one]; any adult present to maintain order and propriety (correct behavior) at an activity of young people

Chaplin, Charlie [CHAP-lin, CHAR-lee] (1889-1977); English comedian and film maker, well known for silent films that linked comedy with pathos; identified with the "Little Tramp" character he created

Chelsea [CHEL-see]; a neighborhood on the West Side of the Manhattan borough of NYC

cicada [si-KAY-da]; an insect famous for making a high-pitched, droning hum

cirrus [SEER-us]; a thin, wispy cloud found at high altitudes

conclusion [kon-KLOO-zhun]; the last part or finish of something that unfolds in time; the end of the story or the summing up of an argument

collage [kuh-LAHZH]; a work of art made from an assemblage of different forms

confirm [kon-FIRM]; to verify

conifers [KON-i-fers]; cone-bearing trees and shrubs like pines, tamaracks, spruces, and Douglas firs; typically of northern forests

conjugation [kon-ju-GAY-shun]; the act of inflecting a verb to show its grammatical role in a sentence

Connemara [kon-ne-MAR-a]; a district in Ireland

conspiracy [kon-SPEER-a-see]; a group with a secret or evil purpose

contempt [kon-TEMPT]; the act of regarding someone as worthless or inferior to oneself or one's standard

contour feather [KON-toor FETH-er]; any of the outer feathers of a bird; a feather that makes up part of the outer body plumage

Copenhagen [KOPE-en-hage-en]; the capital city of Denmark and one of the world's most environmentally friendly cities

cougar [KOO-gur]; American feline also known as a mountain lion or a puma

covalent [ko-VAY-lent]; a form of chemical bonding that is characterized by the sharing of electrons (usually shared pairs) between atoms

crepe paper [KRAPE pay-per]; thin, stretchy, crinkled tissue paper sold in rolls for craft making

cripes [KRIPES]; an expression to indicate annoyance or dismay, similar to "Yikes!"

culpability [KULP-a-bil-it-ee]; guilt

culvert [KUL-vert]; a large drain, usually created by a pipe or metal cylinder, crossing under a road or sidewalk, that allows water to flow along ditches without washing out driveways or streets

D

deciduous trees [de-SID-yoo-us TREEZ]; trees, such as maples or oaks, that lose their leaves in the fall

decipher [dee-SY-fer]; to interpret or read, especially something difficult

deftly [DEFT-lee]; quickly or skillfully

deist [DEE-ist]; a person who believes, on purely rational grounds, that a god created the universe

de nada [day NA-da]; "it's nothing" in Spanish; a way of saying "you're welcome", or "think nothing of it"

Devils Tower [DE-vils TOW-er]; a dormant volcano in Wyoming

Día de los Muertos [DEE-a day los MUER-tose]; a holiday celebrated by many in Mexico just after Halloween; it brings family and friends together in graveyards to share food and to remember loved ones who have died

Diamond stick matches [DY-mand STIK MACH-iz]; a brand of matches

THE HOWLING VOWELS

digression [dy-GRESH-on]; a change of subject

disciples [dis-SY-pulz]; the most important students of Jesus, according to Christian belief; students in general

dispose of [dis-POZE ov]; to get rid of

ditzy [DIT-see]; silly and scatterbrained

dribble [DRIB-bul]; to move a ball by light bounces or kicks

driving cap [DRY-ving cap]; a kind of warm cap, made of a heavy fabric like tweed or leather, that looks like a refined version of a baseball cap

double-dealing [DUB-ul DEE-ling] (more formally called duplicity); deceitfulness

Dying Swan **[DY-ing SWAN]**; a solo ballet piece created by Russian ballerina Anna Pavlova with choreographer Michel (Mikhail) Fokine after she closely observed the movements of swans in a public garden; the piece is slow and beautiful, and is performed to music composed by French composer Camille Saint-Saens as part of his larger work, The Carnival of Animals; in turn, this piece of music was inspired by a poem by English poet Alfred, Lord Tennyson

E

ecumenical [e-kyoo-MEN-i-kal]; universal; concerned with promoting unity among religions or different movements in the same general religion

Eduardo [e-DUAR-do]; a name meaning "protector"

embark [em-BARK]; to set out on a voyage or adventure

emu [EE-moo]; a flightless Australian bird that resembles an ostrich

enameling [ee-NAM-al-ling]; a glassy, colored, opaque coating fused to a surface to add strength and beauty

engross [en-GROSE]; to occupy exclusively; absorb

Epiphany [ee-PIF-a-nee]; a sudden, deeply meaningful revelation or insight; also, in Christian tradition, the 12th day of Christmas (January 6th), when the Magi or Three Wise Men arrived in Bethlehem

eternity [ee-TURN-i-tee]; a limitless amount of time; sometimes defined as that which is beyond time

evanescent [e-va-NES-sent]; vanishing or fading away, like a soap bubble; fleeting

F

Fays of Destiny [FAZE ov DES-tin-ee]; see Norns

feeble [FEE-bul]; weak

feliz cumpleaños [fe-LEES koom-play-AHN-yose]; "Happy Birthday" in Spanish

flank [FLANK]; to put something on each side of something else

foliage [FOLE-ee-ij]; leaves, flowers, and branches

fractal [FRAK-tul]; a pattern that is repeated at ever smaller scales; a newly invented branch of mathematics

fulcrum [FUL-krum]; the support on which a lever pivots; something that supports; a prop or balancing point

G

Gary [GARE-ee]; a city in Indiana, nicknamed "Magic City of Steel"

Genet, Jean [zhen-AY, ZHON] (1910-1986); a French writer

geometry [jee-AM-e-tree]; a branch of mathematics

ghoul [GOOL]; an evil demon

ginkgo [GINGK-go]; a tree native to China that has fan-shaped leaves; considered a living fossil

gluten-free [GLOO-ten FREE]; without wheat, barley, or rye; these grains all contain the protein gluten, which some people are allergic to

gnome [NOME]; one of a fabled race of dwarflike creatures

goony [GOO-nee]; foolish or awkward, crazy in a fond sense

Gore-Tex [GORE teks]; a waterproof and breathable fabric trademarked by W.L. Gore and Associates

Gorgon [GORE-gun]; in Greek mythology, any of three monsters having snakes for hair; the most famous Gorgon was Medusa

gorgonzola [gore-gun-ZOLE-a]; a pungent Italian cheese, a little like bleu cheese

gothic architecture [GOTH-ik AR-ki-tek-chur]; pertaining to a style of architecture originating in France in the 12ᵗʰ century

gouache [GWASH]; a water-based form of paint and chalk used by artists

gourd [GORED]; a hard, inedible fruit frequently used as harvest decorations; when hollowed and dried, gourds can be used as drinking and storage vessels

gravity [GRAV-i-tee]; a phenomenon in which objects attract one another

green around the gills [GREEN a-rownd the GILZ]; an expression meaning ill or nauseated

grey (gray) [GRAY]; color between white and black; there are two accepted variants for spelling this color, Alexa prefers *grey* because it visually flows into the word *eyes* when typed

grimace [GRIM-us]; a sharp expression of the face showing disgust or contempt

guild [GILD]; an association of craftsmen

groaning board [GRONE-ing BORED]; an old-fashioned and whimsical term for buffet, a table heaped with a feast

H

hamstrings [HAM-stringz]; tendons found behind the knee

hand bell choir [HAND bel kwire]; a group who plays music using the synchronized ringing of hand bells

hand-eye coordination [HAND-AI ko-or-di-NAY-shun]; the coordinated control of eye movement with hand movement to accomplish physical or athletic tasks

hasta luego [ahst-a loo-AY-go]; Spanish phrase meaning "see you later", "until we meet", or "until we meet again"

Hatfield House [HAT-feeld hows]; a country house in England built in 1497 by the Bishop of Ely under Henry VII

helium [HEE-lee-um]; the lightest of all the elements, with atomic number 2, represented by the symbol He; used as a lifting gas in balloons and airships

hellion [HEL-yun]; a rowdy or troublesome person

herbaceous [er-BAY-shus]; regarding a green plant with leaves and stems (and possibly flowers) that dies down to the ground at the end of the growing season; includes annuals and perennials

hija adorada de [EE-ha ad-dore-AH-da day]; "adored daughter of" in Spanish

Hitchcock, Alfred [HITCH-kok, AL-fred] (1899-1980); a celebrated director of suspense films

Hod [HAHD]; in Norse myth, he was the blind brother of Baldur; he was tricked by Loki into killing his brother with a missile of mistletoe

hola [O-la]; "hi" or "hello" in Spanish

Houdini, Harry [hoo-DEE-nee, HARE-ee] (1874-1926); a magician from Hungary who specialized in the escape arts

hypnotic [hip-NOT-ik]; inducing sleep or an unconscious state that is like sleep

I
Iago [ee-AH-go]; a character in Shakespeare's play *Othello* who hates Othello for passing him up for promotion; considered an incarnation of irrational evil

immoveable [im-MOOV-a-bul]; permanently fixed in place

impetuous [im-PET-choo-us]; marked by sudden and forceful emotion, speech, or action

inadvertent [in-ad-VER-tent]; unintentional

incredulous [in-KRED-zhoo-lus]; disbelieving; skeptical

Indian corn [IN-dee-an KORN]; a colorful variety of dried corn used as a harvest decoration

indigenous [in-DIJ-a-nus]; native to a particular place

infinitesimal [in-fi-ni-TES-i-mal]; immeasurably small

inhalation [in-ha-LAY-shun]; the act of breathing in (as opposed to exhalation, the act of breathing out)

innovate [IN-no-vate]; to introduce something new

insignia [in-SIG-nee-a]; a distinguishing sign, similar to a logo

insinuating [in-SIN-yoo-ay-ting]; making suggestive remarks designed to provoke doubt

interconnectedness [in-ter-kon-NEK-ted-nes]; a worldview which sees a oneness in all things

intrigue [in-TREEG]; to arouse the curiosity of; also to scheme or plot

Iron Girl [AI-urn gurl]; Alexa's spinoff on a song by the British heavy metal band Black Sabbath called "Iron Man"

irresistible [eer-e-ZIST-a-bul]; incapable of being withstood

Isabelle [IZ-a-bel]; a name meaning "God's promise"

J

Jackson, Michael [JAK-son, MY-kel] (1958 to 2009); American singer who became a star during the 1980s; creator of the moonwalk dance

jeez [JEEZ]; used to express annoyance

Jesus [JEEZ-us]; the central figure of Christianity

K

Keillor, Garrison [KEEL-lor, GARE-is-son] (1942-present); American radio personality and author, originally from Minnesota

King, Stephen [KING, STEE-ven] (1947 to present); American author, screenwriter, film producer and director known for horror stories

knobby [NOB-bee]; adjective form of knob; something that sticks out and is rounded, like a knee or a door knob

L

languid [LANG-gwid]; slow; showing little or no animation or movement

Lao Buddhism [LAO BOO-dis-um]; the type of Buddhism, a religion, mostly practiced in the Asian country of Laos

lasso [las-O]; a loop of rope designed to be thrown around a target and tightened when pulled, typically used to rope cattle

laser [LAY-zir]; a device that emits light through the stimulated emission of photons; lasers are powerfully focused beams of light than can be used in many ways, from cutting metal to performing delicate surgery to creating colorful shows of lights

Last Supper [LAST SUP-per]; in Christian belief, the final meal that Jesus shared with his followers

Laurium [LAO-ree-um]; a town in Greece that in classical times was controlled by Athens and famous for mining the silver was used for coins that supported the Athenian navy and empire; for the slaves who did the mining, being sent to Laurium was a death sentence

laws of motion [LAWZ ov MO-shun]; three physical laws that form the basis for classical mechanics

lens [LENZ]; a piece of transparent material, such as glass, specially shaped to focus rays of light; used in cameras, projectors, glasses, and other optical devices

leukemia [loo-KEE-mee-uh]; a serious blood disease

level [LE-vel]; a flat, horizontal surface; evenly; or story of a building.

lexicon [LEK-si-kahn]; a list of words in alphabetical order; a dictionary or glossary; sometimes used to describe the personal and preferred vocabulary of a speaker or writer

linden [LIN-den]; any of various shade trees of the genus *Tilia* having heart-shaped leaves

literal [LI-ter-al]; exact or taken in a non-figurative sense

The Little Mermaid [the LI-tul MER-made]; a fairy tale by Danish author Hans Christian Andersen (1805 to 1875)

The Little Tramp [the LI-tul TRAMP]; a silent movie starring Charlie Chaplin about a tramp who is wily and bumbling but usually good-hearted and trying to behave like a gentleman (see "Chaplin, Charlie")

llama [LAH-ma]; a domesticated South American mammal prized for its wool

Loki [LO-kee]; from Norse myth, Odin's blood brother and resident of Asgaard; honorary god of discord and mischief who was overcome by Thor

Lookout Mountain [LOOK-owt MOWN-ten]; a mountain in three different U.S. states

Lorre, Peter [LOR-ee, PEE-ter] (1904 to 1964); a Hungarian-American film actor who specialized in portraying scary or monstrous characters

luge [LOOJ]; a winter sport in which participants race feet-first downhill on toboggans

Lutheran [LOO-ther-an]; a follower of the Protestant Christian denomination named for Martin Luther

luxury [LUK-zher-ee]; something inessential but providing comfort or pleasure

M
mahogany [ma-HOG-a-nee]; numerous varieties of dark-colored, reddish-brown hardwood

Mall of America [MAL ov a-MARE-i-ka]; a huge shopping mall in the Twin Cities suburb of Bloomington that is built around an indoor amusement park

Mandelbrot, Benoit [MAN-del-brot, buh-NOYT] (1924 to 2010); French-American mathematician who coined the term "fractal"

manic [MAN-ik]; frenzied, intense

masquerade [mas-ker-ADE]; to go about disguised or in costume; to pretend

mausoleum [MOZ-o-lee-yum]; a tomb; a structure made to house human remains after death

mercifully [MER-si-ful-lee]; fortunately

Merman, Ethel [MER-mun, ETH-al] (1908-1984); singer, known for a powerful voice, who appeared in many musical comedies on stage and in movies

metropolis [me-TRA-po-lis]; a large city or urban area, usually with more than a million people

MGM [EM JEE EM]; a filmmaking studio in Hollywood, California; the initials stand for "Metro-Goldwin-Mayer"

millennium [mi-LEN-nee-um]; a period of time equaling 1,000 years, usually meaning from, for example, the year 1000 to the year 2000, but also meaning any period of 1,000 years

MINN [MIN]; abbreviation for Minnesota, a state in the Midwestern United States; Postal abbreviation MN

mint condition [MINT kon-DI-shun]; having excellent, new-like quality

MIT [EM AI TEE]; abbreviation for Massachusetts Institute of Technology, a famous engineering school

montage [mon-TAHZH]; a filmmaking technique which uses rapid editing and music to present compressed information, similar to a collage

moonwalk [MOON-wok]; a kind of dance step in which the dancer seems to be sliding on the spot and defying gravity

Mount Rushmore [mownt RUSH-more]; a peak in South Dakota that has Presidents Washington, Jefferson, Lincoln, and T. Roosevelt carved into its face

mugger [MUH-ger]; one who makes exaggerated faces; also, oddly, someone who robs a pedestrian

muggy [MUH-gee]; sticky, humid (related to weather)

myth [MITH]; a traditional story, especially one concerned with deities or gods

N

nano-biceps [NA-no BY-seps]; a term Alexa made up to suggest one billionth of a bicep (the main muscle in the arm); in other words, muscles so tiny as not to exist

Narcissus [nar-SIS-sus]; in Greek mythology, a hunter renowned for his handsomeness; he was proud, and fell in love with his reflection in a pool

naturalmente [na-choo-rahl-MEN-tay]; "naturally" in Spanish

Navajo [NAH-va-ho]; the second largest Native American tribe in North America, renowned for their artistry in weaving, pottery, and silver-smithing

Newton, Sir Isaac [NOO-ton, SUR AI-zik] (1643 to 1727); a British physicist who famously worked with gravity, motion, and optics

Niagara Falls [ny-AG-ruh FALZ]; collective name for a trio of powerful waterfalls which form part of the border between Canada and the United States

nonplussed [non-PLUST]; puzzled

Norns [NORNZ]; female beings of Norse mythology who rule the destiny of gods and men; they are giantesses; also called Nornir or Fays of Destiny

Nornir [NORE-neer]; see Norns

NYC [EN WY SEE]; the abbreviation for New York City

NYU [EN WY YOO]; the abbreviation for New York University, a private research university based in New York City

O

obligatory [ah-BLIG-a-to-ree]; required or mandatory

oblong [AHB-long]; shaped like a rectangle, oval, or elongated sphere

obsolete [ahb-so-LEET]; no longer in use

Odin [O-din]; the major god in Norse mythology, sometimes compared to Zeus in Greek mythology and called "the father of the gods"

Odyssey [AH-de-see]; the younger of the two surviving ancient Greek epic poems (the older is the *Iliad*); it tells the adventures of the warrior king Odysseus as he struggles to return home after the Trojan War and of his wife, Penelope, and son, Telemachus, as they struggle to keep the kingdom of Ithaca safe during Odysseus' twenty-year absence

of yore [ov YORE]; from long ago

opaque [o-PAKE]; not allowing light to pass through; dark or not well understood

osteoporosis [os-tee-o-pore-OH-sis]; a common disease in which bones become subject to fracture and heal slowly; prevalent in older people

Otto [AHT-to]; a name meaning "wealth"

outstrip [owt-STRIP]; to surpass or be better than

P

pantheon [PAN-thee-on]; the Greek for "all gods"; a set of all the gods of a particular religion

parabola [pa-RAB-o-la]; in mathematics, a section of a cone; often used to mean an arc similar to the shape of a rainbow or horse shoe

parentheses [pa-REN-the-sees]; curved punctuation marks used to set off information from the main sentence

par excellence [par ek-se-LAHNS]; a French expression meaning the best or truest of a kind; quintessential

pathos [PA-thos]; a quality of speaking or writing that arouses pity or compassion

Pavlova, Anna [PAHV-lo-va, AH-na] (1881-1931); famous prima ballerina from Russia

peewee [PEE-wee]; something that is especially small

penny whistle [PEN-nee WI-sul]; a simple six-holed woodwind musical instrument

Peter, Paul, and Mary [PEE-tur, POL, and MA-ree]; American folksinging trio that made its debut in the 1960s

pewter [PYOO-ter]; a metal mostly made of tin

pilgrims [PIL-grimz]; early settlers of Massachusetts who were from England

pinner cap [PIN-er kap]; a small cap trimmed with a ribbon bow, pinned to the hair with hairpins, popular in the 1700s

pin oak [PIN oke]; a deciduous tree having small acorns and lobed leaves

Pipestone [PYP-stone]; a city in southwestern Minnesota; the site of Pipestone National Monument

pixels [PIK-sels]; dots of color; the basic units of an image on a television or computer screen

poke bonnet [POKE BON-et]; a hat tied under the chin, designed to shield the face and neck from sun, also restricting the vision of the wearer

pore [PORE]; a word with many meanings; Alexa uses it to mean "to stare"

Potter, Harry [hare-ee PAH-tur]; hero of a series of fantasy novels by J.K. Rowling involving adolescent wizards

Presley, Elvis [PRES-lee, EL-vis] (1935-1977); American rock-and-roll singer popular in the mid-20th century

Prose Edda [PROZ ED-a]; an Icelandic collection of Norse myths dating from 1220 C.E. and generally believed to have been written by Snorri Sturlson

punctuate [PUNK-choo-ate]; to mark or divide

pyramid [PEER-a-mid]; a structure where the outer surfaces are triangular and converge at a point

Q
quark [KWARK]; an elementary particle of matter and energy too small to be seen

Queen of Hearts [KWEEN ov HARTS]; a character from *Alice's Adventures in Wonderland* by Lewis Caroll

quizzical [KWIZ-i-kul]; suggesting puzzlement

R
Radio City Music Hall [RAY-dee-o SI-tee MYOO-zik hal]; an entertainment venue in Rockefeller Center, NYC, with more than 5,000 seats for spectators

raffia [RA-fee-a]; a fiber from the leaves of the raffia palm; strands are used for tying objects

ravenous [RA-ven-us]; extremely hungry

rectilinear [rek-ti-LIN-ee-ar]; characterized by straight lines and right angles

regulate [REG-yoo-late]; to put in order, to systematize

resilience [re-ZIL-yens]; the property of a material to absorb energy when it is deformed; the ability to regain original shape after a blow

requiescat in pace [re-KWEE-es-kaht in PA-chay]; a Latin phrase meaning "may she/he rest in peace"

rhythmically [RITH-mik-lee]; of, relating to, or having rhythm; recurring with regular intervals of time

Rice Krispie treat [RYS KRIS-pee treet]; a sweet snack made from Rice Krispies cereal, melted butter and melted marshmallows

ring-around-the-rosy [RING-a-ROWND the RO-zee]; a fun children's game in which the players dance in a circle and then fall down while singing a rhyme from the 14th century

Rockefeller Plaza [RAHK-e-fel-ler PLAH-za]; a complex of commercial buildings in New York City with a skating rink and a roof garden

rousing [ROW-zing]; lively or stirring

rudbeckia [rood-BEK-ee-a]; North American herb with bright yellow petals and brown, cone-shaped flower heads; known commonly as Black-eyed Susan

rye [RY]; a particular grain or the flour made from it; bread made from pure rye flour is dark brown and very dense and flavorful

S

sage [SAJE]; a plant of the genus Salvia which has leaves that can be used as seasoning

sagging [SAG-ing]; drooping

sailor's hornpipe [SAY-lors HORN-pyp]; a traditional melody for the instrument called the hornpipe; also a dance characterized by hopping on one foot at a time

satisfied [SA-tis-fyd]; contented or at ease

Sawyer, Tom [SOY-yer, TOM]; the main character of a novel by Mark Twain, the pen name of Samuel Langhorne Clemens (1835 to 1910); first published in 1876, *The Adventures of Tom Sawyer* was a popular success and has since become a classic of children's literature; Tom is adept at getting into and out of scrapes

Schulz, Charles [SHOOLTS, CHARLZ] (1922-2000); a Minnesota native and cartoonist best known for the long-running cartoon "Peanuts"

Seattle [see-A-tul]; a port city in Washington State, first settled in the 1850s; Seattle is famous for many things, including green landscapes and lots of rain

self-sufficient [SELF-su-FI-shent]; independent

settee [set-TEE]; a small or medium-sized sofa

shackle [SHA-kul]; a metal fastening for confining the ankle or wrist of a prisoner; chains

sherry [SHER-ree]; a Spanish wine, or a wine made elsewhere to imitate it

Shrek [SHREK]; an animated film from 2001 featuring Mike Myers as the voice of a large, green ogre named Shrek

sieve [SIV]; a utensil for straining or sifting

silverback [SIL-ver-bak]; a mature male gorilla having silvery hair across the back; any mature and dominant mammal

skittish [SKIT-tish]; restlessly active

ALEXA'S LEXICON

slouchy [SLOW-chee]; to hang carelessly; to slump

Snoopy [SNOO-pee]; the beagle belonging to Charlie Brown in the classic comic strip "Peanuts." To be *snoopy* means "to be nosy," and Snoopy is very well-informed and has a large snout (see Schultz, Charles)

snowshoe hare [SNO-shoo hare]; a species of hare found in North America; it is named "snowshoe" because of the big size of its hind feet and the marks its tail leaves

solar [SO-lar]; relating to the sun

spruce [SPROOS]; any of various evergreen trees having drooping cones and bluish-green needles

Squanto [SKWAN-to]; sometimes called Tisquantum, he was the Native American who assisted the Pilgrims after their first winter in the New World.

Stentor [STEN-tor]; a loud-voiced Greek herald in the *Iliad,* an epic poem

stentorian [sten-TOR-ee-an]; extremely loud

stern [STERN]; a rear part or section

Stratocaster [STRAT-o-kas-ter] (also called Fender Stratocaster); a model of electric guitar made from 1954 to the present

sub-par [SUB-PAR]; not measuring up to the standard

suede [SWAYD]; leather with a soft napped surface or a fabric made to resemble it

sumac [SOO-mak]; any of various shrubs having red fruit and pointed green leaves that become scarlet in autumn

summarize [SUM-a-ryz]; to make a summary of or to express concisely

summit [SUM-mit]; the highest degree that can be attained; also the top of a mountain (and therefore the highest point around)

superheat [SOO-per-heet]; to heat excessively or overheat

sustain [sus-TAYN]; to keep in existence; to preserve

Swiss Army knife [SWISS AR-mee nyf]; a brand of multi-function pocket knife

synopsis [si-NOP-sis]; outline of a plot

synthesize [SIN-the-syz]; to combine different materials or ideas together into a new orderly whole

T

tableaux [tab-LO]; a vivid description; a living picture

tactful [TAKT-ful]; considerate and discreet

taffeta [TAF-fe-ta]; a smooth, often shiny, woven fabric made from silk or synthetic fibers

tarnish [TAR-nish]; to discolor, especially by exposure to air or dirt; discolor of a metal surface caused by corrosion or oxidation

tarragon [TER-i-gon]; an aromatic herb

terrapin [TER-uh-pin]; a North American family of turtles that live in the water

tentative [TEN-ta-tiv]; uncertain; subject to change

terra-cotta [TER-a KAH-ta]; a brownish orange color typical of unglazed earthenware garden pots

terra incognita [TER-a in-kog-NEE-ta]; a Latin term used in cartography for regions that have not been mapped or documented; it literally means "unknown land"

texture [TEKS-chur]; the feel of a surface

Tibetian prayer flags [ti-BET-un PRAY-yur FLAGZ]; small, colorful, rectangular flags of paper or cloth, usually block-printed with designs and prayers and strung in groups on string; in Tibet, prayer flags hang outside where the wind can flutter them and activate the prayers for peace and prosperity for all living things

tongs [TONGZ]; gripping and lifting tools used for picking up hot food

topcoat [TOP-kote]; a heavy coat worn in winter

topography [ta-PAHG-ra-fee]; graphic representation of the surface features of a place on a map, indicating their relative positions and elevations

Toyota Prius [toy-O-ta PREE-us]; an amazing hybrid electric car; it was the first mass-produced hybrid vehicle

translucent [tranz-LOO-sent]; allowing light to pass through

triple trio [TRI-pul TREE-oh]; group of nine singers (three trios) singing *a cappella* in close harmony

trip wire [TRIP wyr]; a wire stretched close to the ground that activates something when tripped over, like a trap; a form of booby trap

Trollheim [TROL-hym]; in Norse myth, where the trolls dwelled

truffle [TRUF-ful]; any of various edible fungi of the genus Tuber; essentially a rare, flavorful and expensive mushroom

Twin Cities [twin SI-tees]; nickname for Saint Paul and Minneapolis, together comprising the largest urban area in Minnesota. St. Paul is also the state capital. Those who live nearby call them "the Cities."

U

unadorned [un-a-DORND]; not decorated; plain; simple rather than elaborate or complicated

Urd [OORD]; a goddess of fate in Norse mythology, one of the three Norns; a giantess who personified the past

Ursula [UR-soo-la]; a name meaning "little she-bear"

usher [USH-er]; to escort

V

vegan [VEE-gan]; a strict form of vegetarianism; someone who does not eat any animal products, including meat, dairy, fish, eggs, and honey

vegetarian [vej-uh-TARE-ee-an]; someone who does not eat meat

vessel [VE-sel]; a craft designed to navigate on water or a hollow utensil such as a cup

vid [VID]; short for video

Viennese [vee-en-EEZ]; the variety of German spoken in Vienna, Austria

virulent [VEER-oo-lent]; extremely poisonous, infectious, or dangerous

vitae [WEE-ty or VEE-tay]; derived from the Latin word "vita" meaning "life"; a form of academic resume called more formally a "curriculum vitae"

W

wage [WAJ]; payment for services to a worker, especially on an hourly, daily, or weekly basis; earnings in exchange for labor

The Walt Disney Company [the WALT DIZ-nee KUM-pa-nee]; one of the largest entertainment corporations in the world; it specializes in family entertainment, animation, and theme parks

wing chair [WING chare]; a kind of upholstered armchair with a high back and curved arms like wings on each side

Wise Men [WYZ men]; also known as the Magi; in the Christian tradition, a group of three distinguished astrologers who are said to have followed a bright star or comet to discover the birthplace of Jesus shortly after his birth and present him with homage and precious gifts

Wonder Bread [WUN-der BRED]; the name of a made-up musical group from Sundog, Minnesota; more commonly, a brand of enriched white bread noted for its colorful packaging guaranteeing freshness and bland taste appealing to children

Wonder Woman [WUN-der WU-man]; a DC Comics super heroine, created by William Moulton Marston in 1941, loosely based on the Greek idea of Amazon women warriors

Y

Yankee [YANG-kee]; an inhabitant of New England or the United States

Yggdrasil [IG-dra-sil]; in Norse mythology, Yggdrasil was a gigantic ash tree, sometimes referred to as "the world tree," that aligns the nine worlds of the Norse cosmology

yurt [YERT]; a tent used by nomadic peoples of Asia

young'un [YUNG-un]; an informal expression meaning "a child"

Z
zinc [ZINGK]; a metallic chemical element that is bluish-white and somewhat brittle or chalky

Zoliath [zo-LY-ath]; made-up version of the name Goliath

Zorro [ZOR-ro]; Spanish word for "fox"; the literary character of a masked swordsman who defends the weak; Zorro first appeared in a 1919 novella by Johnston McCulley called *The Curse of Capistrano* and has been the focus of many television shows, movies, and comic books since

Read other books from Do Life Right, Inc.!

Lisa M. Cottrell-Bentley

Wright On Time®

Book 5

MINNESOTA

Illustrated by Tanja Bauerle

Go on the road with homeschoolers Nadia and Aidan Wright as they travel cross country around the U.S.A. going to all 50 states. Each book takes the kids to a new state with a new fun and educational theme, all while trying to solve the mystery of the strange Time Tuner device the family finds in their first adventure in Arizona. Explore caves in Arizona, a dinosaur dig in Utah, alternative energies in Wyoming, a newspaper in South Dakota, and sculpture gardens in Minnesota.

Cody Greene and the RAINBOW MYSTERY

WRITTEN BY LINDA FIELDS

When a painting is stolen from nine year old Cody Greene's family's art gallery, he does what any artist does best: he sketches the clues. Through cooking with his friend, visiting the midwife with his mom, hiking with his dad, and helping to prepare for an upcoming art and craft festival, Cody's homeschooling takes a new turn as he unravels the Case of the Rainbow Mystery.

Write a book with Monica and Julie! When two homeschooling best friends team up to enter a novel writing contest, things get busy fast! Through planning for birthdays and getting ready for Halloween, Monica and Julie's writing adventure becomes one novel concept!

ABOUT THE ILLUSTRATOR

Heather Newman has been drawing since she was big enough to hold a pencil, and her prized possession as a young girl was a large box of blank essay books, perfect for writing and illustrating stories or drawing her own images for favorite stories. Creating art continues to bring her great joy over 30 years later! Her work has ranged from murals to pencil portraits to books, but her favorite projects have always involved artwork for children. Heather used watercolors for the cover of Howling Vowels and pencil for the interior illustrations. Heather was the primary illustrator in the children's chapter book, *Cody Greene and the Rainbow Mystery* (published in April 2011, Do Life Right, Inc.).

After spending a little over a year having many grand adventures traveling the country in an RV with her family, Heather found her dream home in the woods of Maine. She lives with her wonderful husband, three amazing, homeschooled sons, two friendly mutts and one slightly grumpy cat.

Heather and her work can be found at:
www.heathernewman.net

ABOUT THE AUTHOR

Leslie Schultz is a lifelong artist intrigued by subtle connections between stories and images. She likes exploring how to tell stories not only with words but with photographs. Leslie began writing stories and poetry in third grade. Today, she has published poetry, fiction, essays, interviews, and book reviews, and she makes her living as a writer helping non-profit organizations. In addition, Leslie carries her camera everywhere, and she exhibits and sells her photographs.

As a child, Leslie moved extensively with her family, living in many states and overseas. Consequently, she always longed for roots. Now, Minnesota is her home. Here, along with her husband, Tim, and daughter, Julia, she revels in the turn of the seasons, the connections with neighbors, and the ongoing adventure of homeschooling. At first, homeschooling seemed a daunting prospect, but she knew that what Julia needed couldn't happened in a school setting, and so Leslie decided to take a leap of faith. Now, Julia has a tailor-made program of stimulating academics balanced by fun with friends and time to dream and create.

The Howling Vowels grows out of this experience of homeschooling in a small Minnesota town. As Julia began reading, she couldn't find any books about other children who were homeschooled. Leslie began writing the book for Julia, and Julia encouraged her to publish it.

Learn more about Leslie by visiting:

www.winonamedia.net

COMING IN 2012!

And Sometimes Y

A sequel collaboration of *The Howling Vowels* by
Leslie Schultz and Julia Braulick

Three years have passed. In Alexa's home of Sundog,
Minnesota, the Howling Vowels are reunited after
Ursula's long stay in Ireland. Life is good for these lively
'tweens but things are unsettled by the disturbing
presence of a new boy, Yves. Is he a potential friend? Or
a volatile and even dangerous intruder? Follow Alexa
and her friends—Eduardo, Isabelle, Otto, and Ursula—
as they ride horses, train dogs, make magic on film and
stage, and struggle to understand the vagaries of the
human heart.

Made in the USA
Charleston, SC
21 December 2011